The Shadow Called William

By

Orlando R. Zapata

Contents

Preface

You Will Read in This Book

Across these pages, you will experience the journey of a young boy growing into adulthood — guided by an imaginary character who made a real difference in his life and in the world.

What began as imagination eventually became reality as he grew older and made contact with an alien world.

I hope you enjoy the story as you read these pages. I wrote this book in plain English, easy to follow and understand.

— Orlando R. Zapata
U.S.A. Citizen, born in Colombia, South America

Prologue

You will enjoy this fascinating work of historical fiction. As you read, you may feel as though you are transported to a different place. Some of the characters may even let your imagination carry you to another planet.

At times, imagination takes us far into journaling and reflection, creating the sensation of stepping outside the world we know. These journeys of thought may lead us in different directions, shaping our lives in unexpected ways. In this story, you will find a character who can travel with ease beyond space and into new worlds—always guided by God and protected by guardian angels.

Remember, this is a work of fiction. It is only the imagination of the author, inspired by places that may or may not exist, and it should not be mistaken for real history.

Her aunt, Mrs. Emma Louis, with a new warehouse, doubled her business by adding more merchandise. Her mother, Evelyn, slowed down and avoided too much movement because her osteoporosis had worsened. She sold her old house and moved to Limoges, into a large home that she had reconstructed. Now they lived closer to downtown. When her mother became sick, Doctor William admitted her to the hospital for a week until she recovered and was discharged. They visited her every two weeks.

Nolan Phillis proved to be a good businessman. Mr. Ross, the wealthy engineer, admired him because of his serious and disciplined character. It had been three years since Nolan had opened his engineering offices, and during this time, he had earned good money. He was a devoted son who loved his parents and always stayed close to them.

Now he had taken his parents on vacation to Italy, where some relatives lived. In his absence, Mr. Ross's secretaries managed the office until his return.

Nolan had been with his girlfriend, Lilian Penelope, since high school. She was a beautiful, petite woman with striking blue eyes that matched his own. Nolan, tall and thin at 5'7, was a handsome man and very approachable, always easy to talk to. Recently, he had received a brand-new truck—a four-wheel drive—from his brother, William, as a graduation gift. It was exactly what he needed as an engineer.

Nolan adored his nephew, William Jr., and never visited without bringing him new toys. The little boy, equally fond of his uncle, was deeply spoiled by the entire family. Sometimes, his grandparents took him to their house, where he had everything a child could dream of. At four years old, he already read small children's books. His adopted grandparents, Mr. Carlos II and Mrs. Virginia, loved him dearly and often called him "Little William," predicting he would grow up to be just as smart as his father.

Tatty, William's wife, loved her son immensely. She often took him to the Galaxies, where her only brother lived. Tatty's parents had died in the war when she was five, but her sister and husband raised her, giving her an education that eventually led her to become a general doctor in the Galaxies. Every month, she worked for a few days in the Galaxies Hospital before returning to Earth. During her time away, William Jr.'s grandmother cared for him. Though she split her life between two worlds, Tatty was happy to be married to Doctor William on Earth.

Doctor William also assisted in the Galaxies whenever their hospitals received an overwhelming number of patients with heart problems.

Meanwhile, Evelyn, William's grandmother, was hospitalized again after suffering complications with her heart and worsening diabetes. The insulin treatments were no longer effective. Desperate to help, Doctor William injected her with a special medicine from the Galaxies. Though it gave her a little more time, her heart remained too weak, and her condition was critical. The family—his mother and aunt especially—were heartbroken, sensing her days were short.

One day, while returning from a surprise trip to the U.K., Doctor William landed his helicopter in the laboratory's parking lot, where a landing space had been arranged for him. The captain of the French Air Force, John Robert, was waiting to inspect the helicopter, having received alerts from central communications that a suspicious aircraft had entered the area. William provided his FAA documents, but the captain insisted on checking inside. What he didn't know was that a Galaxy's mechanic was hidden inside, performing maintenance on the spaceship systems disguised within the helicopter. During the inspection, the mechanic transformed the interior to appear like a normal military helicopter. Convinced, the captain apologized, saying he only acted on an alert, and left in his own helicopter. William and the mechanic later laughed during their flight back, knowing how close they had come to exposure. The advanced ship had automatically doubled its speed earlier because it was connected to the pilot's mind, and William had been anxious about being late to his meeting, triggering the alert.

Beyond his medical work, Doctor William also cared deeply for the homeless. Curious to see their lives firsthand, he once disguised himself in old, dirty clothes and wandered downtown, accompanied discreetly by his drivers for protection. He sat on a bench, where a homeless man named Peter offered him coffee. They walked together to a small restaurant that provided free coffee and sandwiches to the homeless. William, calling himself "Jony," shared a meal with Peter and listened to his tragic story—how Peter lost his young wife and unborn child to medical complications, which led to his downfall into alcoholism and life on the streets. Peter praised Doctor William, unaware that he was speaking to the man himself, for providing meals through his charities. The encounter moved William deeply, reinforcing his mission to continue helping those in need.

Soon after, Evelyn's health declined further. Despite William's efforts, even a heart transplant could not save her fragile body. Surrounded by family and under constant care from nurses, she passed away peacefully at home after suffering greatly during her earlier years in the German camps of the Second World War.

Her funeral was held at Louyat Cemetery. During the service, Doctor William spoke briefly but with deep emotion:

"Today, we say goodbye to my grandmother. Though we are saddened by her departure, we believe she has passed into a better world than this one. Her life was filled with hardships, but also with love. She may be gone from our sight, but she will forever remain in our hearts. May the Lord receive her soul."

The family then returned home to support Mrs. Lorena, who was overcome with grief. Later, Mrs. Emma Louis gathered everyone at a hotel for dinner to remember Evelyn's life together.

Doctor William had two patients scheduled for heart operations. One of them was his adopted grandmother, Mrs. Virginia Alberton, who had recently been slowing down in her social life. She often felt tired and short of breath. After examining her, William determined that she needed heart surgery.

Jack reassured the family with his strong faith, while William prepared for the operation. Mr. Carlos II spoke to William, saying, "William, take care of your grandmother. She loves you so much." William replied, "Well, Grandpa, you know better. I love her too, but I have faith in the Lord that she will recover."

Though he wished he could take her to the Galaxies for the surgery, he knew that was impossible. Instead, he brought back advanced medical equipment from the Galaxies to assist with blood circulation during operations. This machine did not exist in any Earth hospital. William discussed it with Dr. Jean, head of the hospital, explaining that the equipment would only be here temporarily until production for hospitals on Earth began. Dr. Jean agreed, but required William to sign documents releasing the hospital of any liability should something go wrong. William accepted, knowing he had access to other advanced medical equipment as well.

Three days later, engineers from the Galaxies delivered the machine to the hospital. They appeared human, so no one realized they were from outer space. William first tested the equipment on another patient, Mrs. Theresa Robles. The operation took much less time than expected, and her recovery was also faster. The equipment proved easier to clean and disinfect, making the entire process smoother.

The other doctors at the hospital were astonished. The hospital's owner called William, asking when the equipment would be available for mass production, though they suspected it would be expensive. William told them he couldn't provide a timeframe but promised to update them when production was ready. Naturally, no one knew that the company manufacturing the equipment was based in the Galaxies, with some parts produced there and others assembled on Earth. William had even set up a local plant to help supply hospitals with these parts.

Virginia Alberton was admitted to the hospital for her heart valve surgery. William and his wife Tatty, who was also his nurse, operated together. It went smoothly without complications. Afterward, Virginia was moved to the recovery room where her family waited.

When William emerged from the operating room, Jack, his adopted brother, gave him a big hug, followed by their grandfather. "This is my boy," the old man said proudly. "The first day I saw him, I knew he was part of our family." The entire family cried with happiness, including William himself.

William preferred that Tatty continue to care for Virginia in the hospital because he did not trust the other nurses, despite their professionalism. He feared they might accidentally give the wrong medication.

Around this time, Nolan Phillis returned from vacation, bringing gifts for everyone, including a special one for his nephew. He and his parents visited William's house. Mrs.

Lorena was overjoyed to see her grandson and his wife again. During their visit, William received a phone call from Jack.

"Hi Jack, how are you?" William answered.
"I'm fine, thank you," Jack replied. "My mother said we may gather this afternoon at my parents' home. If you could bring your family, it would be wonderful."

William asked his parents, who had just returned from a trip, and they agreed. "It's settled then," he told Jack, who happily confirmed.

News of William's success spread quickly, and newspapers now called him *Doctor William, the inventor of advanced heart equipment.* The engineers from the Galaxies created a second machine for organ operations, and demand for the technology grew rapidly. To meet production needs, Earth engineers had to be trained in advanced electronics, as much of the technology was far beyond their current capabilities. William even built a new factory to produce electronic parts, hiring Japanese engineers skilled in electronics.

While Earth was only beginning to modernize its electronic systems—moving from hot radio tubes to transistors—the Galaxies had already achieved fully automated technology. This gave William a massive advantage. With two factories producing medical instruments and hospital equipment, he became a multi-millionaire in a remarkably short time.

Some businessmen grew suspicious, wondering if William was actually a spaceman or an alien. In truth, his intelligence was extraordinary, with an IQ likely over 140. He had funded his entire medical education himself, but few understood the real source of his success. At one hospital meeting, Dr. Braun openly suggested that William must be from space. Though not exactly correct, the idea was closer to the truth than anyone realized.

The Alberton family later celebrated their fiftieth wedding anniversary, attended by many prominent businessmen. During the celebration, Mr. Carlos II proudly introduced William to everyone. In his speech, he explained how important his decision had been fifteen years earlier to adopt William into the family.

"Don't think he was homeless or in need," Carlos said. "He was a humble young man, a medical student with a big heart, always ready to help anyone. Even today, if he sees someone in need, he will stop and help. That is why our family loves him. He has even taught me lessons I never passed on to my own children—the value of giving love to strangers. We grew up with everything, but he showed us the world outside of privilege."

The room erupted in applause, and William's parents were moved to tears by the words. Jack also spoke, proudly calling William his brother. The party lasted late into the night.

Meanwhile, William's medical office was thriving. Though he personally only performed heart operations, the office was staffed with skilled doctors he had trained and paid generously. He always supported them whenever they needed help.

Mrs. Lorena planned to retire in a year, and William, as CEO, prepared her replacement well in advance, ensuring proper training before she stepped down.

William Jr., now eight years old, attended St. Michael Catholic School. The school had recently added a bus service, but often the Governor's wife personally picked him up and dropped him home. Twice a week, he trained with a personal fitness coach near his father's exercise area. Bright and hardworking, he earned good grades in school. He often rode his bicycle to his grandparents' home, only two blocks away, where he enjoyed his grandmother's cooking and spoiled affection.

One day, while looking at an old military photograph in her room, he asked his grandmother about his late grandfather. She explained that he had been a U.K. Air Force pilot during World War II, flying B-17 bombers alongside the Americans. In the 1943 Münster raid, his plane was shot down. He bailed out, but his parachute malfunctioned before opening, leaving him badly wounded. After the war, he worked at an aircraft parts company for twenty years before retiring and later passing away peacefully in his sleep.

"Do you miss him, Grandma?" William Jr. asked.
"Of course I do," she replied gently. "But we must learn to let go and find peace in remembering."

From a young age, William Jr. believed the Galaxies were simply another country, as no one explained the truth until he was older.

Meanwhile, Mrs. Lorena reconnected with long-lost family. She had a sister in Spain, but recently discovered a half-brother she never knew existed. His name was Christian O'Connor, her father's son from a previous marriage.

Christian shared his harrowing story: during the war, he had been imprisoned in Germany. To escape being sent to a

camp, he faked a self-inflicted wound to be taken to the
nurse's office. There, he overpowered the nurse, tied her
up, and ambushed two soldiers one by one, killing them
and taking their uniforms. Using their keys and a nearby
jeep, he managed to escape. Speaking fluent German, he
blended in as he walked past soldiers, eventually reaching a
port where he abandoned the jeep and fled to safety.

Christian had an uncle named George, who owned tour
boats. Late one night, around three o'clock in the morning,
Christian arrived at his uncle's house near the Waterport
and knocked on the door.

When George opened it, he was startled. "What are you
doing here at this hour?" he asked.

"Uncle George, please help me," Christian pleaded. "I just
escaped from the Germans. Yesterday, at Barum
Transportation Company, the German soldiers waited
outside until the day's work ended. As everyone left, they
handcuffed every Jewish worker, myself included. I spoke
to them in German, and they told me that once we reached
the prison, they would speak to the Captain and set me free.
They lied. They locked us all in prison—that was four days
ago."

George stared at him. "How did you escape from them?"

Christian held up his arm. "I cut myself, and they sent me
to the infirmary. The nurse stitched me up, but once she
was finished, I overpowered her. I gagged her, tied her
hands, and locked her in the restroom. After that, I killed
two soldiers—one at a time—and ran. I took a jeep that was
parked outside."

"Did you bring the jeep here?" his uncle asked.

"No, I ran about a mile and a half to get here. I left the jeep outside the Waterport."

George shook his head. "You're a smart boy. The Germans are probably searching for you all over town. We don't have much time. I'll take you to the Island of Groix, in Morbihan. It isn't very populated, and you can hide there. I also know someone who can change your passport to an English one. He owns fishing boats and can hire you as a mechanic. Give me your savings card or bank book. Tomorrow, one of my workers will withdraw all your money, leaving just the minimum balance."

Christian replied, "Uncle, I also have a security box at the bank. But I don't have the locker keys. They were with my things when the Germans arrested me. The company I worked for is owned by people from the U.K., so maybe the Germans won't shut it down. The business is important—transportation between the U.K. and France."

"Perhaps it's still open," George said. "Tomorrow, we'll send someone there to retrieve what's in your locker. For now, I'll take you to a friend's house. Tomorrow night we'll go to the island, and from there you'll get a small boat to Groix. Once the passport is ready, you can board one of the cruise boats to South America. Stay there until the war ends."

The next day, German police—the Gestapo—were already searching for him at the Waterport. They even showed his passport photo to people in the area. George, realizing the urgency, sent one of his employees, Mr. Richer, to Christian's workplace. When Richer arrived, he saw German soldiers in the parking lot.

One of them asked, "Do you work here?"

"No," Richer replied calmly. "I'm a businessman in the transportation industry." He entered the office, where the secretary greeted him.

"May I help you?" she asked.

"I'd like to speak with Mr. Schaffer," he said.

"Please wait, I'll let him know," she answered.

Ten minutes later, Mr. Schaffer entered, noticing Richer's briefcase. "Good afternoon, sir. What can I do for you?"

Richer introduced himself. "I work for Mr. George Patty."

"Oh yes," Schaffer nodded. "He owns the cruise boats. I know him."

"I'd prefer to speak privately," Richer said.

"Of course," Schaffer agreed, leading him into his office and closing the door. "Now, what's this about?"

Richer explained, "Four days ago, the Germans arrested Mr. Patty's nephew right outside this building. He's now in prison. Mr. Patty has asked me to retrieve the contents of his nephew's locker. The Germans took everything he had on him, but the locker may still hold his personal belongings. His wife could use them."

Schaffer thought for a moment. "Let's ask the secretary. I know there's a spare set of locker keys."

The secretary confirmed this, retrieved the duplicate key for locker #30, and handed it to Schaffer. He personally went to open the locker, then returned with a large bag containing everything Christian had stored there.

"Thank you," Richer said, taking the bag. He returned to George's office, where they found the savings book and checkbook inside.

"Richer," George said urgently, "we don't have much time before the Germans reach the bank and freeze his funds. Take this authorization paper, signed by Christian, and withdraw everything."

Richer hurried to the bank, presented the signed document, and the teller verified the signature with the records. After a brief wait, the teller retrieved the money from the vault and asked, "What denominations would you like?"

"Large bills," Richer answered. The teller complied and also brought out the contents of safety deposit box #32. Richer placed everything into his briefcase and left.

As he exited the bank, two Gestapo officers entered. Wasting no time, Richer climbed into a pickup truck and sped away. By the time he returned to George's house, he had secured all of Christian's belongings.

Later, Christian recalled, "My uncle helped me. After I received my new passport, I traveled to South America—to Brazil—and I have lived here ever since. I have a son here, though I haven't seen him in about a year."

Lorena listened with tears in her eyes as her half-brother finished. "I want to return to France someday," Christian said softly. "When I do, I'll let you know."

"Goodbye, brother," Lorena whispered, crying as they parted ways.

Chapter 1: The Boy Who Chased Butterflies

Every child, at around five years old, dreams up an imaginary friend or creature. Some invent animals; others breathe life into toys. Few realize it, but the sharpest among them are guided by what feels like a sixth sense.

This is the story of one such boy.

Once upon a time, in a humble South American village near the mountains, a woman named Lorena lived with her young son, William. The families in the village were poor, and most of them were fishermen. Lorena's life had been marked by loss; her husband had abandoned her shortly after William was born, and her own family lived far away in another country. Yet she refused despair. Strong-willed, resourceful, and proud, Lorena promised herself she would one day be independent.

Though she worked tirelessly as a seamstress, fate had blessed her with a found family who cared for her as their own. A kindly grandmother figure adored Lorena as if she were her daughter, and neighbors often welcomed her and William. Still, loneliness pressed heavily, and she missed her husband dearly.

Lorena rented a tiny house, its wooden doors and windows neatly painted, its fence simple but sturdy. In the yard sat the shell of an old Younker car—no wheels, no doors, no seats. Its steering wheel clung stubbornly to the rusting frame. For William, it was a kingdom.

The little boy spent hours inside the husk of that car, gripping the wheel, imitating the growl of an engine only he could hear. It became his world of adventure. His mother, sewing dresses inside, would check on him often, calling him in for meals, coaxing him into afternoon naps.

One day, as William played as usual, something magical happened. A cluster of butterflies fluttered into the yard. Their colors shimmered in the sun, reds, blues, yellows, and they circled him, landing gracefully on the windshield frame. Enchanted, William ran inside.

"Mother! Come see!"

Lorena followed him outside. She saw nothing but an empty frame. "Perhaps you'll see it again, William," she said gently, before being pulled away by a knock at the door. Customers had arrived.

But from that day forward, the butterflies returned. Every afternoon, William waited in the Younker car, and like clockwork, the creatures danced for him. At first, he only watched. Then he dared to stretch out his hands, giggling as they circled his fingers. To William, it was a secret friendship, a world apart from war and hardship.

Lorena sometimes worried. Was it normal for a boy to be so captivated? His laughter was bright, but it reminded her too much of his absent father, Harry Roberts, brilliant, charming, but drifting, restless, and doomed. Harry had been a mechanic on great ships like the Mauretania and the Queen Mary. But drink, cigarettes, and recklessness had ruined him. Then came the hunting trip in the South American hills. He never returned. Some whispered lions took him, though his body was never found.

Now, watching her son lose himself in butterflies, Lorena feared that same restlessness might live in him too.

Yet William was no ordinary child. At five, he could already read and count. Since children in their country did not begin school until seven, Lorena taught him herself. Neighbors adored him. The Hoopers next door treated him like family, passing food over the fence and begging Lorena to let them build a gate. Mrs. Linda Hooper bathed and dressed him with the same care she gave her daughters. The three girls, nine-year-old Sandy, seven-year-old Lucy, and five-year-old Marsh, often played with William through the small wooden gaps in the fence, their laughter echoing across both yards.

It was the 1940s. There was no television, only books, coloring pencils, and imagination. For William, the butterflies became companions. For Lorena, they were both a comfort and a warning.

War, however, had other plans.

Lorena had been born in Strasbourg, and the German invasion scattered her family. With Harry gone, she returned to France with William, finding work in a makeshift hospital. She leaned on her brother Oliver for help. William was placed in a Catholic school in Limoges while Lorena tended to soldiers broken by the fighting. When she returned to France, her husband's Uncle was dead and left some money to her husband in Manchester.

But shadows grew darker. Deportations haunted the streets. One day, Lorena learned that her mother, Evelyn O'Connor, had been taken east. She refused to abandon her. With William in tow, she boarded a train to Poland, across occupied cities. Soldiers checked her papers at every stop. Her son, wide-eyed, stared at burning buildings as she held him close.

A year after returning to France, Lorena finally discovered the truth about her mother's fate. Determined, she set out once again. At last, in Kraków, Lorena found Evelyn in a detention block. Their reunion was fierce, tears flowing after years apart. Evelyn embraced William too, whispering how his birthmark reminded her of a brother long dead. But joy was short-lived. German soldiers patrolled every corner, their cruelty casual and unpredictable.

That cold night, an officer barged into their room, eyes cold. "Who are you? Why are you here?" Lorena stammered out the truth that Evelyn was her mother. The officer only sneered. "Tomorrow at six a.m., you and the boy will leave. Soldiers will take you to the train. Be sure you're ready."

Morning came heavy with dread. Lorena kissed her mother goodbye, tears streaking Evelyn's cheeks. Then, soldiers forced her and William into a jeep, delivering them to the train station. As the train pulled away, Lorena watched farmland scarred by bombs slide past. The journey stretched endlessly, the train rattling through the darkness all night, its whistle echoing across ruined fields. William rested his head on her lap, whispering, "Are we there yet, Mama?" She smiled faintly, stroking his hair.

By chance, when they finally reached Strasbourg, Lorena met her cousin Jonathan Ford. He had been delivering hospital supplies and recognized her face on the staff board. Against protocol, he convinced a secretary to give him her address. When he appeared at her door, memories stirred of family lost and scattered. They shared grief that his father, Manson, was killed in a bombing; her years in exile.

Jonathan met William, handing him a bag of fruit before returning to his truck. "I'll see you again," he promised, and disappeared down the road.

Lorena stood in the doorway, her son beside her, the echoes of butterflies still alive in her memory.

A few months later, Mrs. Lorena received a long-awaited letter from her mother. Evelyn wrote that the war was finally over and she had managed to escape. She described the confusion of walking alone to the train station, exhausted and unsure of where to go, until a kind stranger recognized her family name, Emma O'Connor. To Lorena's astonishment, her mother had found her long-lost sister alive in Dijon.

By December 1945, the first Christmas without war, Lorena tried to bring normalcy back into her household. She decorated modestly, hosted friends from the hospital, and fielded her son William's questions about Santa Claus with a gentle mix of comfort and realism. The boy, influenced by his schoolmate's Buddhist father, wavered between belief and doubt, while Lorena quietly shouldered both his wonder and his worries.

Soon after the holiday, another letter arrived, this time with her mother's address in Dijon. Relieved, Lorena left William in her brother's care and, traveling by bus, set out to reunite with her family. At her Aunt Emma's house, a tall boy greeted her at the door, leading her to Evelyn, who rushed forward, arms wide. Their embrace was the kind that carried both grief and renewal.

Emma, once a celebrated singer under the name Emma Louisa Schiffer, had built a comfortable life despite losing her husband before the war ended. Her home, large and

well-kept, offered a stark contrast to Lorena's modest
rented house. Yet Emma's warmth made the difference.
Over dinner, she promised to visit Lorena and young
William soon, bridging years of silence with a renewed
bond.

Lorena returned to Strasbourg with a sense of grounding.
Though the scars of war remained, family had been
restored, and with it, the fragile but vital promise of
continuity.

Chapter 2: Shadows of the Father

The years passed, and William was now ten years old. One evening, after returning home from school, he spoke to his mother with a troubled look.

"Today they gave out letters," he said, frowning. "Next June twentieth, the school is hosting a Father's Celebration. Every student's father is supposed to come." He rolled his eyes and muttered bitterly, "Why would they even give one to me? My father is dead."

Lorena set her sewing aside and looked at her son carefully. "What is it, William?"

He hesitated, then asked the question that had lived quietly in his heart for years. "Mom… how did my father really die? Nobody told me exactly. They just say he disappeared while hunting. The police didn't find his body, only some of his things, stained with blood. I've always hoped maybe he's still alive, somewhere in the mountains."

His young voice trembled, torn between hope and anger.

Lorena sighed, her eyes clouding with memory. "The truth, son, is uncertain. The police Sergeant, Johan, told me the Indians up there spoke of caves and geysers that burst across the narrow mountain passes. They found your father's backpack nearly forty feet down from one of those foundations. Nobody just the pack. Some say it was volcanoes, others believe giant lions, creatures that don't belong in this world. The Indians were terrified. American hunters once came to investigate after a small plane crashed in those same mountains. They found nothing—no wreck, no people, no trace of your father. I waited almost a year, hoping for news, but none came. That's why I returned here, to start again."

At that moment, Emily, a young reporter, was visiting the house. She had been listening and finally spoke. "In my three years as a journalist, I've heard many strange stories. But whatever lives in those mountains… nobody has been able to face it yet."

George, another neighbor who had joined them, shook his head. "This is beyond anyone's hands. Something unnatural is out there. If it killed men before, it will kill again."

Lorena placed her hand gently on her son's shoulder. "William, someday, when you're ready, we'll talk about the full truth of your father's story."

She rose and went to the kitchen to finish supper. A knock soon rattled the front door.

"William, check who it is," she called.

The boy opened the door. "Mom, it's Mr. Lucas, our neighbor."

"Tell him to come in. I'll be there soon," she answered.

Mr. Lucas explained that his bathroom drain was clogged. Lorena led him there, and while she returned to cooking, he fixed the pipe. When he was done, he waved away payment. "You've been so kind to my sick wife, Mrs. Lorena. Keep your money, but if you insist, two pounds will do." He left soon after.

William finished eating and asked eagerly, "Mom, can I go play basketball at the park with Richard and the others? I'll be back in an hour."

Lorena gave him a look. "Don't forget you haven't finished your homework."

"I'll do it later," he promised, rushing out.

Not long after, Victoria Boss, the lady across the street, came knocking. Her daughter was very ill. Lorena, ever kind, went with her to help. After examining the girl, she insisted, "She must go to the hospital immediately." Once the emergency was settled, Lorena returned home.

That night, she told William, "Your grandmother and Aunt Emma have arrived in town. They're at the hotel, and they'll come tomorrow morning. We must clean the house tonight."

"Mom! The house is always clean," William protested.

"Your room is not," Lorena countered firmly.

"Alright, alright. I'll clean it after finishing my school project. I want to get it done tonight so I can enjoy the weekend."

The next morning, Evelyn and Emma arrived with Noah, Emma's private driver. They brought gifts, groceries, and warmth. Lorena was overwhelmed with joy to see her mother and aunt again.

Emma shared a painful memory of July 1944, how an airplane had crashed right in front of her car, her husband suffering a fatal heart attack from the shock. She confessed that since his death, she had longed for family. Turning to William, she asked gently, "What do you want to be when you grow up?"

William answered without hesitation. "A doctor. But it's expensive."

Emma smiled. "And what if someone helps you?"

"Then I'll surely do it," he said brightly.

Later, Emma spoke privately to Lorena. "I will cover William's schooling. The church pastor, Father Michael, will transfer the funds through my bank. Your son must have every chance."

Lorena embraced her, tears in her eyes.

That evening, the family attended a grand celebration at the Hotel Ritz Paris. Emma was being honored for the twenty-fifth anniversary of her first hit record, *Moonlight and Sunset*. Guests gathered, music filled the air, and for one night, war and sorrow were forgotten.

When the party ended, Emma made sure everyone had a room to rest in. Lorena tucked William into bed.

"Mom," he said with a grin, "that cake was so good I licked my fingers. I want more."

"Not now, my love. Time to sleep."

The next day, life returned to routine for Lorena at the hospital, William at school. She did the laundry, patched his torn pants, and reminded him to wear his soccer uniform properly. When she discovered he had been spending afternoons at Camila Locksheed's house instead of his aunt's, she confronted him.

"Why didn't you tell me?"

"I was afraid of your reaction," William admitted. "Camila and her family are kind. They even want to visit us after church this Sunday."

Lorena hesitated, then nodded. "Very well. But you must always be honest with me."

William hugged her tightly. "Thank you, Mom!"

Later, he mentioned his soccer team needed new socks and special support gear. "John Miller's father got him good ones from a store in another town. Can we go too?"

"We'll see," Lorena replied. "Tell me more after you talk to John."

That night, William fell ill with a fever from playing in the cold after his game. Lorena gave him home remedies and watched over him, praying his strength would return.

Outside, autumn winds swept the streets, carrying with them the quiet weight of past sorrows and future hopes.

Chapter 3: The Dark Island

On a cool Saturday morning, Camila and Mary Lockhead, cheerleaders from Saint Michael's School, arrived at Lorena's doorstep. Their voices rang with cheer as they praised William's talent on the soccer team.

"He's bound to score in the next game," Mary grinned.

Lorena blinked, surprised. Until that moment, she hadn't realized how good her son had become. The girls invited him out, but William shook his head politely. His grandmother and Aunt Emma were due to arrive, and he would not miss that for anything.

By late morning, Evelyn and Emma arrived, greeted warmly by both mother and grandson. Coffee filled the kitchen with its rich aroma as they gathered at the table. Emma leaned forward, her voice carrying both warmth and authority.

"I spoke with Rector Souder," she said. "He says William is not only clever but also promising in athletics. I want to pay for his studies. And when vacation comes, I'll find work for him in Dijon."

Lorena's eyes welled. "Emma… you cannot know what this means."

Overcome, she wept with gratitude. For a moment, the scars of war and loss softened, replaced by the promise of her son's bright future.

That spring, Saint Michael's soccer team entered the interschool tournament. Their opening match was against the Georgia Academy, a formidable rival. The game was fierce. Georgia struck first, but William answered with a swift equalizer, his shot curling into the net. The crowd erupted. In the second half, he scored again, and Saint Michael surged ahead. The band played, the cheerleaders cheered, and it felt as if the whole town stood behind them.

But then everything changed.

Charging toward a third goal, William was shoved hard. His body slammed into the goalpost, and he collapsed, unconscious.

The stadium fell into silence. Lorena's scream pierced the stillness. The ambulance rushed him away while his mother, grandmother, and Aunt Emma followed in tears.

At the hospital, the doctor's words were measured. "He is not gone," he said gently. "But he is in a coma. Now… we wait."

The Dreaming

Inside that stillness, William dreamed.

Butterflies flitted past his face. Angels shimmered into view, calling themselves guardians. One, with golden hair and kind eyes, spoke softly.

"My name is Ella," she said. "Your team won the match. Robert scored in your place. But you, William, are not dead. You still belong to the living. You must learn what strength means."

William whispered, "Am I… lucky?"

Ella smiled. "More than you know. Your great-aunt Emma loves you as the son she never had. Your God would not want it any other way."

But William's heart carried a heavy question. "Is my father truly dead? Or is he lost somewhere in the mountains?"

Ella's face grew solemn. "That is an adventure we must take." She took his hand, and together they flew. Below them, William saw his own body lying in the hospital bed. Fear gripped him.

"Do you want to know the truth about your father?" Ella asked.

His breath caught. Slowly, he nodded.

The Voyage

They descended upon a ship, cutting through restless seas. Its captain, Alexander Brady, welcomed him with a firm handshake. Beside him stood Jaydon, a strong and watchful man.

"This is Jaydon," the captain said. "He will guide you."

Life on the ship overwhelmed William, sailors shouting orders, storms raging, food laid upon tables grander than anything he had seen. Seasickness claimed him during a violent squall, and the ship's doctor tended him.

He asked a sailor what year it was. The man only laughed. "Could be 1880. Or 1950. Depends on if you're in your right mind."

Jaydon told him they were bound for the Dark Island.
There, whispers said, lay the secrets of William's missing
father. But the sailors spoke too of hostile natives and
beasts that haunted the mountains.

One afternoon, eager to help, William tried fishing with the
crew. A mighty tug yanked him overboard. The sea
swallowed him whole. Desperation clawed at his chest until
Jaydon's strong arms pulled him back. Coughing on the
deck, William looked up to find sailors cheering as though
he'd been reborn.

That night, Ella appeared again in his cabin. "Trust
Jaydon," she said. "Through him, you will find the truth."

By dawn, the Dark Island loomed ahead. Boats lowered
into the waves, carrying men toward the unknown shore.

The Island

"Stay close," Captain Alexander commanded. His voice
shook as he spoke of past accidents and savage beasts.

The men climbed the mountain, sweat streaming in the
blazing sun. They camped by nightfall, cooking turkeys
shot by Dylan, their cook. Vigil was kept in turns, but
William could not sleep.

Jaydon noticed. "What troubles you?"

"I can't rest," William admitted.

"Try," Jaydon said gently. "Tomorrow, we reach the Indian
village. They are friends."

Morning came with the smell of roasting turkey and strong coffee. By noon, they descended into a valley where Indians greeted them cautiously. Samuel, who spoke some of the language, bargained with their leader, Benjamin. Corn, coconuts, fruits, and even deer meat were exchanged for blankets, rifles, and a bottle of rum. Two mules would carry the goods to the beach.

But William felt eyes on him. An old man in the village, silent and watchful, seemed to see deeper than words.

Back in France

Meanwhile, in France, Lorena visited her son's bedside daily. Doctors reassured her. "He is healthy. His blood pressure is strong. He may wake at any time."

Emma Louise pressed them harder. "Bring in specialists. I will pay."

Dr. Wyatt answered calmly. "There is no brain damage. It is only a shock. He can wake at any moment."

Yet a week passed, and still William did not stir.

Blood and Beasts

On the island, two hunters, Joseph and John, ventured into the southern forests with guides named Black Wolf and Half Moon. They hunted deer, only to face tragedy when a leopard attacked. Black Wolf was slain before John's bullets brought the beast down. The salted meat was hauled back to the village, sorrow shadowing the victory.

Meanwhile, storms struck the ship. Captain Alexander fought the helm, turning the vessel east. When an engine failed, men fished for tuna while repairs were made. William, delighted, caught one himself.

At night, campfires flickered, laughter rolled, but William sat quiet, torn between awe and dread. Jaydon noticed. "You miss your mother," he said.

"Yes," William whispered.

"You are stronger than you think."

The Cave of Truth

Their journey pressed deeper into mountains riddled with geysers, caves, and roaring lions. At last, Ella returned, guiding William and Jaydon into a vast cavern. Mist shrouded the place, and in its depths, William saw a vision.

His father is fighting a lion, shooting it through the chest. But another beast came from behind, tearing at his neck. William's breath hitched as he watched lions devour the man. His spirit rose, drifting into light.

Tears streamed down William's face. "So… it's true."

The angel touched his hand. "He is at peace."

The cavern was filled with radiant light. Ella's voice grew softer, fading. "Now, William… it is time to return."

And in that light, William felt himself being carried back toward his body, his mother's voice calling to him.

Chapter 4: The Miracle Boy

When William opened his eyes after five days in a coma, the hospital room filled with tears of joy. His mother, Lorena, hugged him as though she would never let go; his grandmother wept openly. Doctors ran their tests, expecting weakness or damage, but instead found a boy perfectly healthy.

"Some children," one whispered, shaking his head in awe, "are touched by something beyond us."

News spread quickly. Reporters crowded the hospital, but Lorena stood firm: *Not today. Family first.* That evening, William returned home. Neighbors and classmates filled the street with cheers, tables overflowed with food, and laughter carried into the night. Camila, his closest friend, hugged him tightly, trembling as she whispered:

"You're a lucky boy."

Soon his grandparents arrived from Manchester with gifts and tears, and the local paper crowned him **The Miracle Boy of Strasbourg**. But behind the joy, William carried a deeper truth.

Alone with his mother, he finally spoke: of angels, of the ship, of the wild island, and of the lions that devoured his father. Lorena broke down, holding him close.

"At least now," she whispered, "I understand. At least now we know."

Back at School

The weeks that followed revealed change. His teachers noticed he could finish their sentences, answering questions before they were asked. His soccer coach warned him that his kicks were too strong, capable of shattering nets.

Two weeks later came the championship. The stadium pulsed with music, banners, and cheering crowds. St. Michael's fought fiercely, but William rose above all. Calm under the roar of hundreds, he tore through defenders and scored again and again until victory was certain. Lifted on his teammates' shoulders, embraced by his family, he wasn't just a boy who had survived. He was something more.

The Seventh Grade

That week, Lorena was called into the director's office. William sat waiting with his professors.

"Your son is ready," Director Coffman said. "We believe he should advance to seventh grade immediately."

Lorena, proud and steady, agreed. William himself spoke calmly: "I can handle the program."

The following Monday, he began his new classes, carrying both his old curriculum and the new with ease.

Family Visits

Friday night brought another surprise. Lorena's cousin Jonathan arrived with his mother, Aunt Amelia. Tears and embraces followed. They spoke of family lost in

Manchester, of Lorena's mother, Evelyn, in Dijon with
Aunt Emma, and of William's growing seriousness.

That same night, William came home late from church,
where he taught religion to younger children. He teased his
mother about missing chocolate cookies; she teased back
about his endless studies. Yet Lorena's heart grew heavier.
She saw more clearly every day that her son was not like
other boys his age.

The Rumor

One afternoon, neighbors came knocking: a man nearby
could not breathe. Lorena was at work, so William went in
her place. He prayed silently, blessed a glass of water, and
gave it to the man. Moments later, the sick man rose from
his bed, walking unaided for the first time in days.

By morning, rumors filled the street. *The Miracle Boy had
healed him.*

Reporters soon arrived, but Lorena refused them. "He only
prayed," she said firmly. "Anyone can pray."

Behind closed doors, she warned her son: "Do not do this
again. Not for the neighbors. Do you hear me?"

"Yes, Mother," he promised.

Camila's Sweet Sixteen

Summer came, and with it Camila's sixteenth birthday.
Emma arranged for William to work in Dijon, but promised
her driver, Noah, would bring him back for the celebration.

The party was grand: Camila in a princess dress, William in a blue suit. Father Matt blessed the gathering, and William's graceful, well-spoken words led the first toast. Applause filled the hall as he danced the opening waltz with Camila.

But later, she drew him upstairs to her room. "I want to talk about us," she whispered, pulling him close, her lips trembling near his.

William pulled away gently. "Camila… we're too young. We have time. And this is not the right moment, not with your parents below."

She turned away, wounded. The rest of the night, she ignored him, speaking with friends as if he wasn't there. At two in the morning, William thanked her parents with grace, kissed Camila goodnight, and left with his mother.

Love pulled at him, but so did duty.

Emma's Illness

In Dijon, William worked at Emma's store, astonishing customers with his uncanny ability to know what they wanted. But one afternoon, Noah brought troubling news: Emma was ill. William rushed home, found her fevered, and quietly guided his grandmother in preparing an herbal tea. When Dr. Aaron arrived later, he prescribed medicine—strangely, not the one he had intended. William had pressed him, altering the course.

Days later, Emma recovered fully. She never knew how close her heart had been to danger.

A New Life

Meanwhile, Lorena's own life shifted. She moved to a larger hospital in Alsace, bought a new home, and reconnected with old friends. Her laughter warmed patients, her dedication brought her peace.

And one Saturday morning, as she prepared breakfast, a knock came at the door.

William opened it. "Mom," he called, "Doctor Carlos is here."

Lorena, in the kitchen, looked up. Her long chestnut hair slipped loose, the blanket around her shoulders falling slightly as she turned.

Carlos froze, the sight engraving itself on his heart.

Chapter 5: Whispers In the Hospital

One morning, Mrs. Lorena arrived at work as usual. She took the elevator to the second floor, clocked in, and was greeted by Madison Lord, an office worker she knew only in passing. Madison surprised her by asking,

"What time do you take your lunch?"

Startled, Lorena replied cautiously,

"Why do you want to know?"

Madison smiled.

"Nothing's wrong. I'd just like to talk to you. But if you don't want to, that's fine."

Lorena dismissed her politely.

"If you need something, let me know. Otherwise, please don't bother me. I have to get to work."

A Rumor in the Cafeteria

Days later, Lorena sat at lunch with Dr. Carlos, her supervisor in the ER. Madison appeared again, greeting them. When Carlos was called away on an emergency, Madison moved quickly to Lorena's table.

"You're not a maid, you know," she said bluntly. "You can sit here with me. So, are you and Dr. Carlos friends?"

Lorena explained that they worked closely together. But Madison's reply was unsettling. She claimed that two years ago, she had gone out with Dr. Carlos twice, and afterward, he cut ties completely. Then she leaned closer and whispered:

"He has a secret. He killed his wife in a car accident. Someone here told me."

Shaken, Lorena ended the conversation and left the table in silence.

Confronting Dr. Carlos

Three days later, Lorena confronted Dr. Carlos directly.

"Why didn't you tell me about your wife, your child, and the grandparents who raised him?"

Carlos froze, visibly uncomfortable.

"Please let's change the subject."

He refused to elaborate, and Lorena, though deeply concerned, respected his silence.

A Theatre Invitation

Life carried on. Weeks later, Dr. Carlos surprised her with an invitation: two theatre tickets for Saturday night. Lorena hesitated, asking for time to think. She was cautious about leaving her house empty. Recently, burglaries in nearby neighborhoods had unsettled her, and she wanted her son, William, at home before agreeing.

William' Gifted Future

William was no ordinary teenager. Brilliant and hardworking, he was already taking medical classes and preparing for a career in pre-med. By the age of sixteen, he was ready to graduate high school, a milestone his mother and Aunt Emma Louise eagerly prepared for.

Invitations went out. Family and friends traveled from Manchester and beyond. On May 25, 1958, William, dressed sharply in a tuxedo, stood proudly among the honor students.

The ceremony was grand. The school director, Professor Coffman, spoke of fresh beginnings. The Monsignor blessed the students' futures. Finally, William was called forward.

His speech was heartfelt. He thanked his hardworking mother, his devoted Aunt Emma (whom he lovingly called his "second mother"), and his grandmother, who had always spoiled him with love. His words brought tears to many in the audience.

A Gift and a Surprise

Afterward, guests gathered outside the school, showering William with congratulations. Among the gifts was a surprise from Aunt Emma: a fully paid trip to Mont Blanc in the French Alps. William, an avid skater, was overjoyed. His mother, equally moved, thanked Emma warmly.

But Emma had another surprise. She announced a grand graduation party at the Hotel Regent Petite France, the very next evening. Dignitaries, doctors, and even government officials would be in attendance.

William rushed to share the news with his classmates. The celebration had only just begun.

The Graduation Party

By four o'clock the next day, Emma was at the hotel, checking every detail: the tables, the seating, the guest list. At six o'clock, the first limo arrived. William stepped out with his mother, his grandmother, and his girlfriend Camila with her parents. To their surprise, two more limos pulled up, bringing additional guests.

The hotel shone with elegance, and William was stunned by the beauty of the arrangements.

By seven o'clock, the ceremony began. Monsignor Paul of the Catholic Church opened with a blessing:

"Lord, thank you for providing these gifts of human hands. Bless this meal, and bless William on his journey into the future."

After dinner, the Governor of Alsace took the microphone. He spoke warmly of Emma's friendship with his wife and praised William's achievements. He even mentioned how William reminded him that, after graduating from high school, he once dreamed of becoming a lawyer.

The applause was loud and sincere.

Next, Emma took the microphone. Her voice trembled with pride as she spoke of her nephew, whom she considered an adopted son:

"William is not only brilliant, but also humble and humanitarian. This is his first step toward his career, and I know he will be the best doctor. Congratulations to him and to his mother, Lorena, who has worked so hard."

The audience rose in applause.

Finally, William himself took the stage. His face flushed with emotion, tears in his eyes, he said:

"This is the night I will never forget. Not because of the party, but because of the love of two women—my mother and my Aunt Emma Louise. And of course, my grandmother, who has always been my comfort. I love you all."

The room fell silent, then erupted in applause. The celebration carried on until after 1:30 a.m.

Whispers of a Greater Calling

(Here, the narrative shifts hinting at William's unique destiny. His studies at the University of Montpellier, his relentless drive, his encounters with mentors, and even mysterious hints of something beyond ordinary medicine, his "work" that borders on the miraculous.)

At the hospital, his presence was already felt. He was not yet a doctor, but somehow healing seemed to follow him. His grandmother's sudden recovery puzzled even specialists. "A miracle," one said. Lorena, though stunned, quietly believed her son had something extraordinary within him.

William returned to college the next day. His schedule kept him busy, but he came home every two weeks. At school, he worked at the restaurant on Cross Street, just off campus, where he had been promoted to manager. Each day, he spent four hours there, keeping the books, paying the workers, and running the floor.

Some of the college girls whispered about him. They noticed how many credits he was carrying, how much he worked, and how unusual it was for someone so young to manage both. To most of them, he was just another new student, freshly arrived for the new year's classes. They did not know he was only seventeen, nor that his mind worked at a level far beyond theirs. Only William knew the truth about himself, and he kept it that way.

Trouble at Camila's Home

Meanwhile, trouble struck at the home of Camila Locksheed, William's girlfriend. Her father, Asher, had fallen ill. Relatives even traveled from Germany to visit him. On the second day, Camila called Mrs. Lorena at the hospital.

"Mrs. Lorena, do you have William's phone number at the college? I don't."

Startled, Lorena asked,

"What's wrong, my dear?"

Camila's voice trembled.

"It's my father. He's very sick. They're running all kinds of tests, but he's in terrible stomach pain."

Lorena tried to reassure her.

"I'll talk to William tonight. He works in the restaurant on Cross Street. If I can reach him, I'll let you know. Please call me if anything changes."

Camila agreed, though she sounded torn.

"I have to go to school tomorrow, but I'll come to the hospital at noon. Please—tell him."

William Learns the News

The next day, Lorena called her son. She explained Camila's situation. William answered calmly but firmly:

"Mom, tell her I'll call her at the hospital. I have one more day of classes this week. I'll try to come on Friday night. Tomorrow, at three, I'll call her myself. But if you can speak with her before then, let her know."

That night, however, William appeared at the hospital around midnight. Quiet as a shadow, unseen by anyone, he entered Asher's room. He examined the man with skills beyond any doctor's, eased his pain, wrote a note in the staff book, and even prescribed a test on the pancreas. Then, unseen, he left.

The next morning, when Dr. Hunter, Asher's physician, arrived, the nurses were puzzled.

"The night doctor ordered medication and a pancreas test," one explained. "He wore an ER uniform. But…there's no signature."

The hospital director was called. New rules were put in place: no doctor would be allowed to examine a patient without first signing in at the nurse's station. Still, the

mysterious intervention had helped. By morning, Asher
was better.

Mrs. Lorena Buys a Car

At the same time, life moved forward for Mrs. Lorena. She
was about to buy her first car, a 1950s Ford sedan offered
by a doctor at the hospital. Though old, it was freshly
painted and had a fully overhauled engine and
transmission. The mechanic advised her to wait a week for
the papers and her new driver's license expired for four
years, to be in order.

This car would change things at home. She had long relied
on public transportation, though the house had a garage.
William already had his license. Having a car would be a
great convenience.

At the hospital, meanwhile, rumors spread among the
nurses: Dr. Carlos and Mrs. Lorena might soon be a
married couple.

William Comes Home

On weekends, William returned home. He often arrived on
the midnight bus from Strasbourg, tired but happy. One
Saturday morning, he woke early and brewed coffee. When
his mother came downstairs, he hugged her.

"Hi, Mom. I love you."

"Sweetheart, you came home late last night. I heard you,"
she said, smiling.

William explained that the restaurant owner had called in sick, leaving him in charge. He had closed the place himself, paid the employees, and taken inventory before rushing to catch the last bus. The delay meant he didn't reach home until after midnight.

That same morning, Dr. Hunter visited Asher in the hospital.

"Do you remember the doctor who checked you last night?" he asked.

Asher nodded.

"Yes, he was a tall young man. He examined my stomach, pressed here" (he gestured to his side) "the pain was terrible. I must have passed out. Later, I woke up after the nurse gave me pills, and I slept all night. Doctor, that young man looked like…William."

William visited later that day. Asher greeted him warmly, half joking, half serious:

"You know, my boy, the doctor who helped me looked just like you!"

William laughed softly.

"Mr. Asher, I was far from here last night. I'm not a doctor yet. But I'm glad you're feeling better."

Camila and her mother exchanged glances. Her mother whispered,

"Perhaps it was a guardian angel."

Asher agreed, though he remained certain of what he'd seen.

Doubts in Camila's Heart

Camila studied William quietly. She loved him, yet she sensed a distance. He was so mature, so consumed with studies and responsibilities, while she was still young and unsure of herself. More and more, she felt he was slipping beyond her reach.

Family Matters

Life at the hospital kept Lorena busy. One day, she received a call from her cousin Jonathan: his mother, Amelia, was hospitalized with severe respiratory problems. Lorena promised to visit after work.

At the hospital, she found her aunt Amelia connected to machines. Jonathan feared it was lung cancer, though Amelia had never smoked. Lorena remembered that Amelia's late husband, Manson, had been a heavy smoker, and perhaps secondhand smoke had taken its toll. The family gathered Jonathan's sons, Sebastian and Luke, and his own boy, Gabriel, a bright student with a baseball scholarship.

Later, Lorena returned home, weary, only to receive a phone call from William. He reminded her about a green folder he needed for work at the restaurant. Their conversation turned back to Amelia. William asked her to keep him updated and promised to call again.

Strange Healing

That night, unseen, William visited Amelia's hospital room. With instruments no one on Earth possessed, he scanned her lungs, located the tumor, and treated it with a beam of light and liquid medicine. By morning, Amelia was alert and breathing easier, though the doctors were baffled.

Lorena noticed her aunt's sudden improvement and silently wondered. She had long suspected her son was connected to something otherworldly. She had once seen a strange blue light under his door at night. She knew his mind was far beyond his years. But she kept her thoughts to herself, fearing that one day she might lose him to a greater mission.

Love and Confessions

As Amelia improved, Lorena's own life took another turn. Dr. Carlos grew closer to her, and one evening, he invited her to dinner at one of Alsace's finest restaurants. There, he confessed:

"Lorena, I want our relationship to move to the next level."

He revealed his past—his late wife, the accident, and his son being raised by his parents. Lorena listened quietly, then spoke:

"I knew some of this already. But hearing it from you matters more."

They discussed the future. If they were to marry, Dr. Carlos's son would live with them. William, too, would have to accept this new family.

Lorena agreed cautiously.

"First, let's meet as a family. Then we'll see where this road leads."

Amelia's Release

In time, the doctors confirmed that Amelia's illness was not cancer after all. Her lungs showed shadows, but medication improved her condition. Within days, she was discharged, her son Jonathan escorting her home. Yet Lorena knew. She had seen enough to understand that something extraordinary was happening with William, something beyond the reach of any hospital or any earthly science. *"She does not have to travel overnight, we Galaxy people,"* she thought, the words echoing like a secret meant only for her.

Chapter 6: The Weight of Goodbye

The next day, after breakfast, William turned to his mother.

"Mom, how is my Aunt Amelia doing?"

"She is okay," Lorena replied, "but still in the hospital. The doctors were very confused. On her second day there, they said her condition was very bad, her lungs barely working. But then, the very next day, she improved so much that they didn't understand it. They thought some new medicine had worked. They even noticed two strange marks on her back. The doctors said both lungs were now functioning, when only one had been working before."

William smiled softly. "Mom, I prayed for her Friday at midnight. I thought you might have done something, but I am happy my prayers worked for her."

"That is wonderful, son."

He continued, "I also spoke with Aunt Emma Louise. She called me from the college office."

"What did she say?" Lorena asked.

"Not much at first. She just told me she was going home and would talk with me later. But last night she called again and said she'll be coming home today or tomorrow. It's about the college."

"What about it? Did she say anything more?"

"No. But, Mom, do you think I need more money for books? Remember, she helped me a lot when I was in

Catholic school—she paid so much money back then. I was thinking, maybe I could ask her for help again, but this time as a loan. Once I finish and become a doctor, I'll pay her back."

Lorena nodded. "That's a good idea. She truly wants to see you finish your studies. I can see it in her face, she loves you as if you were her own son."

"I know, Mom," William admitted. "Sometimes it feels like she does too much for me. I love her because she is kind, but the truth is, she helps so many students, even those outside this country. I found that out when I worked in her office."

"Son," Lorena said tenderly, "I love you more than anything in this world. I cannot give you what she can, and you know that."

"Yes, I know, Mom. Sometimes it just feels like a handout."

"Well, listen to me," she told him gently. "Talk to her. Let her know you accept her help. She won't mind if you work for her in return during your time off, like spring break. I'm sure she would be glad to pay you. She already told me she trusts you more than anyone else in her company."

"Alright, Mom," William agreed. "I'll call her tomorrow."

"No need," Lorena smiled. "She'll be here tomorrow. I spoke with her last Friday. Tomorrow is visiting day. Dr. Carlos and his son will also be joining us for dinner."

"Wait a minute," William laughed, "you didn't tell me anything about that!"

"She wanted it to be a surprise. While she was speaking with me, she also mentioned her past marriage."

"That's nice, Mom. I'm happy you told me. I'm glad we had this conversation."

"Me too, son."

"Thanks, Mom. Is there more coffee in the pot?"

"No, you'll need to make some."

"Okay, I'll do it," William said with a grin.

Mrs. Lorena was thirty-nine years old, with a fair complexion, blue eyes, and long black hair. She was five feet seven, with a graceful figure and elegant presence. No wonder Dr. Carlos was so deeply in love with her. Her son, William, was tall and athletic, six feet two inches, with black hair, hazel eyes, and a commanding presence. At college, the girls admired him, but unlike most young men, he cared little for attention. His only goal was to finish his medical studies and become a doctor. He was special, though no one truly knew just how different he really was.

On Saturday morning, the front doorbell rang. William was in the living room playing music, while his mother worked in the kitchen.

"William, someone's at the door," Lorena called. "Can you check, please?"

"Yes, Mom," he replied, walking to the door. When he opened it, he was surprised.

"Aunt Emma? What is this a surprise?"

"Hi, William," Mrs. Emma Louise said warmly.

"Come in, Aunt Emma. Hi, Noah, come in, please."

"Hi, William, how are you?" Noah greeted.

"I'm very well, thank you," William answered.

Emma Louise stepped into the kitchen. "Hi, my dear," she said to Lorena.

"Hi, Aunt Emma, how are you?" Lorena replied, smiling.

"Fine, thank you. I spoke to my mother last week," Emma continued. "She has back pain, but she's alright. It bothers her a little. It started when she was in the German camps. She told me they made her lift heavy loads of dirty clothes and even struck her with a piece of wood on her back. Those people have abused so many innocent lives. That's why the international court is working now to hold those responsible for war crimes."

As Emma spoke, William listened closely. "Some people still believe Hitler is alive," she added. "The Americans bombed the building where he was hiding, but some think he escaped Europe. I hope they catch him someday."

Emma then turned to Lorena. "Well, did you talk to William about college?"

"Yes," Lorena said. "Let's bring him into the kitchen."

She called him, and William came in and sat down.

"My boy," Emma Louise began, "your mother and I have been talking about your medical studies."

"Yes, she told me," William said. "I really appreciate everything you've done for me. Sometimes I feel bad. I wish I could repay you a little. What I was thinking is if my mother could get a loan from you, then once I graduate and become a doctor, I'll repay it. Would that be okay with you?"

"Listen, my boy," Emma said kindly, "you do whatever makes you happy. I am here to help you. Medical college is not cheap. I've already arranged everything with my accountant so that three thousand pounds will be ready for each year of your studies."

"Thank you, Aunt Emma," William said gratefully.

"It's alright, my boy. Now, you work in a restaurant, don't you?"

"Yes, I do."

"Well, save that money for your personal needs. Your mother cannot do too much for you, and this way I feel good helping you."

"This summer, I'll be working for you as much as I can," William promised.

Lorena then asked, "Aunt Emma, would you like to stay here for the rest of the day? Dr. Carlos and his son will be joining us tonight for a dinner celebration."

Mrs. Emma smiled. "Whose birthday is it today?"

"Nobody's," Lorena said softly. "Dr. Carlos asked me to marry him."

"Congratulations!" Emma exclaimed, moving close to hug her tightly.

"Lorena, are you cooking potatoes?" she asked, glancing at the stove.

"Yes"

"Stop," Emma said. "Let me call the hotel. They'll prepare the dinner and deliver everything, including service."

"But Aunt Emma, that will cost a lot of money," Lorena objected.

"Don't worry. This will be my first wedding present for you."

Lorena hugged her. "Thank you so much. What time should they come?"

"Around five. We'll serve dinner at six. The hotel staff can arrive around four, if that works for you."

"Perfect," Lorena nodded.

Emma picked up the phone and dialed. "Hello, this is Mrs. Emma Louise Shaffer. Can I speak to the manager in charge?"

"Yes, just a moment," the receptionist said. A pause, then a man's voice came on.

"Hello, Mrs. Emma. This is George Rallies. What can I do for you?"

"George, I need a dinner for seven people delivered to a private home."

"What kind of dinner would you like us to prepare?" he asked.

"Well, George, something similar to the last dinner I ordered two months ago."

"Of course. Our kitchen has the customer list. Where should we send it?"

"This dinner is for a lady named Lorena Roberts," Emma said.

"We'll need her address."

"It's in the new community outside Strasbourg. I'll send Noah to the hotel with the details."

"What time should dinner be served?"

"Five o'clock."

"Then we'll send a driver at three-thirty, and I'll personally follow him to the house," George assured.

"Fine, George. I appreciate the favor."

"Would you like the bill sent to your office?"

"That's fine. Thank you. Goodbye."

Emma hung up and turned to Lorena. "Everything is arranged. Now you'll have plenty of time to get dressed and prepare yourself. Your mother will arrive about two, and Noah will bring her. Dr. Carlos said he'll be here around three-thirty. Everything will be perfect."

Lorena saw Dr. Carlos standing by the front window and went to open the door.

"Good afternoon," said Dr. Carlos. "Hi, Lorena. This is my son, Nolan."

"Hi, Nolan, nice to meet you," Lorena replied. "Well, come in."

William came out of the living room. "Hi, Dr. Carlos."

"William, this is my son, Nolan."

"Hi, Nolan," William greeted. "Do you want to come upstairs and see the rest of the house?"

The boy smiled happily and followed William to the second floor. Meanwhile, the catering staff arrived and began preparing everything for the dinner, ready to serve at five o'clock.

That weekend was a joyful and fortunate one for Lorena and William, filled with hope for a better family life. Lorena and Dr. Carlos planned to marry in December, close to Christmas.

About two weeks later, Lorena received a phone call from her ex-mother-in-law, Mrs. Elizabeth Roberts.

"Lorena," Elizabeth said urgently, "Brayden is very sick."

"Oh no," Lorena gasped. "What is wrong with him?"

"The doctor says it's his heart. He's in the hospital."

"Is he there now?"

"Yes. Today is Friday."

"Well, William is returning tonight from college," Lorena said. "You know we're only two hours away by train."

"I know," Elizabeth replied. "Let us talk tonight with my son, and I will call you tomorrow."

"Alright. I'll talk to you tomorrow. Have a pleasant day. I'll pray for him tonight. Goodbye."

Lorena had already made weekend plans with her fiancé, Dr. Carlos, but now she needed to change them. She would have to speak with him about possibly traveling to Manchester.

The next day, William returned home late at night. Lorena told him about his grandfather's illness.

"Mom," William said, "if you can't travel to my grandparents' house, don't worry. I'll go and spend time there, then return to school on Monday."

"But, William, you're in college," Lorena said.

"Mom, I'll call the college. They'll understand. This is a family problem. I'll work hard to catch up on Monday's classes. You know I'll do it."

"Well, I think that's a good idea. Thank you, son. I only have Saturday off this week because one of the nurses is on vacation."

"Don't worry, Mom. I live next door to the train station. I'll get ready now. I'll see you on Monday. Just let me know when you get there."

"I will, son. Have a good trip."

"Thank you. Take care of yourself. Bye, Mom."

Just as William was leaving, Camila Locksheed arrived at the house by surprise. She ran up to him, hugging and kissing him.

"Hi, dear!" she said.

"Camila! How did you get here?" William asked.

"My dad is in the car outside. My aunt Natalie you met at my house, lives near your grandparents. Her husband plays golf with your grandpa. She called yesterday and told me about him."

"Thank you, sweetheart," William said. "I'm heading to the train station for Manchester."

"Well, if you want me, I'm ready to go too," Camila said quickly. "My aunt will be waiting for me as well. Is that okay, Dad?"

"Yes," her father replied.

Lorena came to the door and greeted Camila. "Come inside. Tell your dad to join us."

William walked to the car. "How are you, Mr. Asher?" he asked.

"I'm fine, my boy. How is school? Do you want to come inside?"

"Yes, thank you," William said.

They all gathered in the house. After a few minutes, William said, "Well, I'd like to catch the ten o'clock train. It's almost an hour's ride by bus to get there."

"No, my boy," Mr. Asher said, "I'll drive you to the train station."

"Thank you, Dad, you're so sweet," Camila said, smiling.

She turned to Lorena. "Goodbye, Mrs. Lorena."

Lorena laughed. "Alright, you two, get ready. Time is running out."

Everyone laughed together, said goodbye to Lorena, and left.

By then, summer was nearly over. Dr. Carlos later took Lorena to the Strasbourg beaches, where they spent the whole day until midnight before returning home, since Lorena had work the next day. Nolan, Dr. Carlos's son, had quickly grown attached to Lorena, accepting her as a mother figure. He even wanted to have a sleepover at her house before returning to his grandparents' the next day.

Lorena and Dr. Carlos were deeply happy. To them, this was a good sign for their future together.

Two months later, Lorena and Dr. Carlos were married in a grand celebration at a private club. Their honeymoon was short; they spent one week in Mexico.

Back home, their plans turned toward building a large house. Dr. Carlos already had a contractor ready to begin construction. There was only one adjustment: previously, Nolan's grandfather had taken him to school every day, but now Dr. Carlos had to handle the school runs until proper transportation could be arranged for his son.

Meanwhile, William arrived at his grandparents' house. After paying for the taxi, he walked to the door with Camila. His grandmother, Elizabeth, greeted him warmly.

"I'm so glad to see you, William," she said, hugging him.

"Now everything will be better with your grandpa," William replied.

Elizabeth explained, "He's in the hospital. We had to take him back."

William already knew about his grandfather's condition. "Okay, Grandma. After a quick shower, I'll go to the hospital. It's about half an hour away."

"It won't take me more than ten minutes," he added.

Camila said, "I also need to go to my aunt's house."

Elizabeth nodded. "Your Aunt Julia was here around one o'clock. She asked if you had arrived with my grandson. I told her you were on your way. If you walk two blocks, there are taxis available. She lives about twenty minutes from here. Her husband sometimes comes to pick up my husband for golf."

"I'll walk with you," William offered.

"Sure, girl," Elizabeth said.

Just before William and Camila were about to leave, there was a knock at the door. It was Julia with her older son, Theodore.

Elizabeth opened the door. "Come in. This is Camila, and this is my grandson, William."

Theodore stepped forward. "So this is William? I've been told you look like your father."

William smiled. "How are you, sir?"

"I'm fine," Theodore replied.

Julia asked Elizabeth, "How is your husband in the hospital?"

"He's on a support machine. He doesn't speak. The doctors are monitoring his heart and will probably give him medication for blood circulation," Elizabeth explained.

"Camila, are you ready?" Julia asked.

"Yes, Aunt Julia."

They left together. William called after her, "I'll see you tomorrow."

He then went to take a shower. When he came out, he said, "Grandma, I'll be ready soon, so you and I can go to the hospital to see Grandpa."

"Okay, dear," she said, "but you must eat something first. I made lunch earlier, thinking you would be here by then."

"No, Grandma. I couldn't. Last night I arrived home late. I took the bus at seven and reached the house by nine. This morning I didn't wake up until nine o'clock. But the most important thing is that I'm here to see Grandpa."

"I know, sweetheart," Elizabeth said.

Just then, there was another knock at the door. William answered it and found a man standing there.

"You must be William," the man said.

"Yes," William replied.

"I'm your Uncle Jaxson."

William nodded. "Yes, I remember. I was about seven years old. How are you, Uncle? My father told me about you."

Elizabeth was in the kitchen serving food to William. As William and Jaxson entered, Jaxson greeted his mother warmly, kissed her forehead, and sat down.

"Would you like something to eat, son?" Elizabeth asked.

"Thank you, Mom. I just ate a sandwich at home, but I'll take a cup of coffee if you have one."

They all sat at the table.

"Mom," Jaxson said, "we need to go to the hospital now. It's after four. We have to meet the nurse and see Father."

"I'm ready," Elizabeth said.

"Do we need to take public transportation?" William asked.

"No," Elizabeth said. "My son has a car."

Together, they left for the hospital. At the same time, Camila and her Aunt Julia were also on their way.

Thirty-five minutes later, William, his grandmother, and Uncle Jaxson arrived at Mr. Brayden's hospital room.

William sat beside his grandfather's bed. He gently took his hand and checked his pulse.

"Would you mind if I prayed for Grandpa alone?" he asked softly.

His grandmother and uncle quietly stepped out of the room.

William checked his grandfather's pulse and, with his medical knowledge, knew the heart was failing. Gently, he placed his hand over the old man's chest and applied a small amount of his special medication. When finished, he disposed of the remnants in the hospital waste bin and draped a cloth over the area.

Moments later, Mr. Brayden stirred, his eyes opened, then closed again. He touched his forehead, then opened his eyes once more and kept them open. Though he could not yet speak, there was awareness in his gaze.

William stepped out of the room and said, "Come in, Grandpa has his eyes open."

Grandma immediately called for the nurse, asking if the doctor was nearby. The nurse entered just then to administer medication. William watched closely as she placed the pills in his grandfather's mouth, already calculating how long the effect would last when combined with the treatment he had given. He estimated one hour, and he was right.

An hour later, the doctor returned. After examining him, he announced, "His heart is working a little better today, but his blood pressure is still very low. He does need a heart transplant. At present, only one hospital in Germany has performed that operation successfully last year. For now, we'll continue treatment here for another week. He must take several medications."

Tears streamed down Elizabeth's face. The doctor placed a hand on her shoulder. "You must have patience," he told her gently.

Then, to everyone's surprise, Mr. Brayden spoke. "I need water," he said faintly.

The doctor quickly removed the ventilator and placed an oxygen mask over him. Soon after, Mr. Brayden whispered, "William, come close to me. I love you, my son."

"I love you too, Grandpa," William replied, tears filling his eyes. He knew there was nothing more that anyone could do except perhaps a miracle.

The nurse brought fruit juice, and Mr. Brayden drank a little.

At that moment, Camila, William's girlfriend, entered. She said, "My aunt wonders if you would like to have dinner with our family tonight."

"Yes, I would," William answered. "I'll take public transportation."

Uncle Jaxson interjected, "No need. I'll give you a ride. Here's my home phone number—call if you need a pickup. Your Uncle Freed also has a car. You won't have a problem getting back."

"Thank you," William said. "Please tell your aunt I'll be there. What time is dinner?"

"Six-thirty," Camila replied.

William turned to his grandmother. "Grandma, you know I love you and Grandpa. But his heart is too weak—he's eighty-eight years old. We must be ready for his passing and for the burial. Only a miracle can save him. Please, Grandma, be prepared. I know it is hard, but I love you."

Elizabeth wiped her tears. "William, my son, you must get ready for dinner. It's already past five. Jaxson is upstairs; he will take you there. It's only ten minutes away by car."

William nodded. "I just need to change into a clean shirt and a nice tie."

"Go to your grandfather's closet," Elizabeth said. "He has a dozen brand-new ties and shirts. If one fits you, take it. They're all new."

"Thank you, Grandma," William said. "I'll take one—my shirt is too plain for dinner."

The next morning, William boarded the train back home. By Monday night, he had returned to college. But there he received an urgent message from the Galaxies: they had been invaded by outsiders. The conflict was fierce, but the Galaxy's people prevailed and built an even stronger society, with more advanced homes, technology, and hospitals. They had even elected a new governor.

William knew he must travel there again, this time to the new Galaxies, a million miles from the old ones. He called his mother. "I'll stay on campus this weekend. I'll be busy," he told her.

She replied, "Your grandpa is out of the hospital now."

That weekend, William traveled to the Galaxies. He spent his time in the hospitals there, caring for the sick. The technology amazed him far beyond anything on Earth. Treatments required no scalpels or physical contact. Doctors used advanced X-ray lasers, and their hands never touched the patient. Their medications were decades ahead of Earth's.

William trained with the Galaxy doctors and was already considered a full doctor there. Yet on Earth, he had to continue as a student, blending in with the others. In truth, he knew more than any medical student alive. On Earth, he had become the number one student in every medical college ranking. Newspapers interviewed him and called him a "genius." His college even announced that all his studies would be fully funded.

In his fourth year of medical school, William worked in the teaching hospital. Experienced doctors tested him with complex cases, and he often performed surgeries that even senior physicians hesitated to attempt. Once, he completed a difficult hernia operation.

Dr. Carlos, his stepfather, said privately to Lorena, "Our son has a superpower brain. We've been married four years, but I never told you before, I thought you might not believe me. William is already a doctor, and the newspapers call him a genius. He is the top medical student in the country. His practical experience is unmatched."

Lorena listened, torn between pride and fear. She thought angels might be guiding her son, but deep inside, she worried such brilliance could mean a short life.

William's experience in the Galaxies was vast operations using magnetic fields to stimulate the brain, transferring power from one body to another without physical touch. Their technology made Earth's medical science seem primitive. Their spaceships traveled faster than the wind, their factories and homes were fully automated, and their energy systems were a million times stronger than solar power. Food was precooked with devices more advanced than microwaves, and even water was produced through powerful machinery.

Earth's military authorities had long suspected the existence of advanced civilizations. Rumors of strange beings, some described as green, others as grotesque, circulated, but much was imagination. William's reality, however, was different. His story was unique. No one truly knew whether he was entirely human or something more.

Meanwhile, Nolan, Dr. Carlos's son, was also thriving. Inspired by William, he excelled in school and became the number one soccer forward in his league, earning a university scholarship. Dr. Carlos had also played soccer in college, and he was proud to see his son follow in his footsteps.

William had once played soccer too, for two years in college, but gave it up to focus on medicine. Now he did not need scholarships. He chose instead to complete his medical studies in just three years instead of four. His time in the Galaxies gave him knowledge no one else possessed.

Already, his destiny was clear: he would graduate as a doctor far ahead of his peers, carrying with him the secrets of two worlds.

Chapter 7: The Double Life of William

One Friday afternoon, William was at the train station, waiting for the six o'clock train to go home, when he saw an old man collapse onto the floor. There were many people at the station, and everyone was staring, unsure of what to do. William quickly stepped forward to check on the man. He took his arm and asked the crowd to give him space.

After examining him, William realized the man was having a heart attack. He immediately began performing CPR. By the time emergency services arrived, the man was already regaining consciousness. William helped him up and walked with him to a nearby bench, where they both sat down.

One of the ambulance staff approached and asked, "What exactly did you do? He seems stable already. Better that we take him to the hospital for observation for at least twenty-four hours. He had a heart attack. Who are you?"

William replied calmly, "I'm a medical college student."

The man pressed further, "How did you know it was a heart attack?"

William shrugged slightly and said, "Just a guess."

The paramedics took the old man to the hospital anyway. After examination, the professional doctors noticed a mark on his arm where it looked like he had received some kind of blood-thinning medication. While checking through the old man's coat pocket, they also found a letter. That was how they learned his name: **Carlos II Alberton**.

When Mr. Alberton woke up, he asked both William and the hospital staff, "What happened to me?"

They explained that he had suffered a heart attack at the train station. Looking at William, he said, "Thank you, my boy."

The staff later informed William that Carlos II Alberton was related to **King Louis XVIII**, and that he had been invited to his uncle's castle for the anniversary celebration of the king's death in 1824. The castle had since been preserved by the governor as part of French history. William himself had once visited the place on a school tour and remembered the artifacts and books about the castle's past.

Out of gratitude, Mr. Alberton offered to help William with his college expenses. But William politely declined, explaining that he was in a good economic position and able to manage his studies.

Still determined to do something, Mr. Alberton said, "I have my business in the U.K. — a shoe factory, among other ventures. Before I collapsed, I had just returned from a meeting in the parking lot with a man from Germany about parts needed for my sewing machines. That stress is probably what triggered my heart attack. They told me at the hospital that it was you who saved me at the train station. They even noticed a small injection mark in my arm. Did you give me some kind of medication? Whatever you did, it helped me. Before the attack, I had high blood pressure, but now it is normal."

William replied carefully, "Sometimes that happens. Maybe one of your veins opened up more after the episode."

Mr. Alberton smiled and said, "Well, I want to do something for you this Christmas. It will be a surprise. I believe I am well now, and you don't need to do anything in return. My family is well-off economically, but still — let me do this. And please, can I meet your family?"

"That is not a problem. I will call home to talk to my mother if she is available this weekend. If she is, give me a call. I wrote my phone number on this business card — it's my home number, not business. Now, it's time for dinner. We need to drive almost half an hour to Alsace."

The nurse called Mr. Carlos's son, saying a limo would arrive in about fifteen minutes to take him downtown. Soon, John, the driver, entered the waiting room.

"Mr. Carlos, how are you?"
"OK, John, let's go home." He then turned to the driver and said, "This is Mr. William, he is my Guardian Angel."

"Nice to meet you," John replied. "By the way, Mr. Carlos, where do you want to go?"
"Not home, I am hungry."
"Ok, sir. And you, Mr. William?"
Mr. Carlos smiled and said, "John, after dinner, you will take me home."

They arrived soon after. Mr. Carlos II pointed at a large building.
"This is my business, Hotel Cour du Corbeau. They cook very delicious food."

"Wow," William said, surprised. "This is a big hotel!"
"Yes, my boy. It is one of the best hotels in the area. We have guests from all over the world."

As they entered, a bellboy approached.
"Mr. Carlos II Alberton, someone is waiting for you inside."
"Who?"
"I don't know, sir."

Inside, his son greeted him warmly. "Father, how do you feel? I am hungry!"

At a nearby table sat a man already having coffee. He stood to greet them.
"Mr. Carlos II, the man you were waiting for, has passed away at the train station in Germany."
"How?"
"He was waiting for the train when two men ran past, hitting him and pushing him onto the tracks. He had no

time to move before an express train struck him. He died instantly."

"I'm sorry to hear that," Carlos said.
"My name is Nicole, and I represent Singer Sewing Machines in Germany. Here is my card. The main office called me today, and since I was only five minutes from here, I came right away."

Carlos nodded. "I'll see you tomorrow at ten o'clock in my office."
"Yes, sir. Goodbye."

Later, William told Mr. Carlos, "Around eight o'clock, I'd like to get back to college. I can't be home too late."
"No problem. Josef, my driver, will take you. But first, let's have dinner."

During the meal, Mr. Carlos sighed. "I have a problem. My niece, who lived near Alsace, disappeared two years ago. We've had detectives searching for her."
"What is her name?" William asked.
"Lily Alberton. She is very thin, slender, about five-foot-five."
"I'll ask some friends. If I hear anything, I'll call you."
"There's a reward of two thousand pounds. The money is already set aside in the bank."

After dinner, William said, "I had a great day, but I need to return to college."
"Of course, my boy. You could be my grandson," Carlos said warmly.
"Let me check your heart before I leave," William suggested. He noticed shortness of breath and asked him to remove his coat. With his stethoscope, he listened to his

lungs. "Send your son, or your driver, to the pharmacy for this medication. I'll wait until it comes."

Carlos agreed. Soon, his son Jack returned with the medicine. The pharmacist confirmed it was good, saying, "The doctor who prescribed this must be skilled." William instructed, "Take two tablespoons a day."

Jack smiled. "William, I'll drive you to college. Dad, go home, take the medication, and rest."
"Ok," Carlos replied. "My adopted grandson — I'll see you soon."

In the car, Jack said, "My father is not usually friendly with anyone. Many try to take advantage of him. But he likes you. He even said he wants to help fund your studies."
William smiled. "I can feel he is sincere."

Jack continued, "If you have time, you should meet my mother and stepfather. They are wonderful people. Do you play any sports?"
"I play soccer," William said, "but not this year. Medical school and hospital practice take all my time."
"You're practically a doctor already," Jack laughed.

They soon reached the college. Jack handed William an envelope. "My father asked me to give you this."
"Thank you," William replied.

When William entered his dorm, his roommate was with a girl, so he left for the library. There, he was met by visitors from Krypton of the Galaxies — his doctors, Pratt and Ratts, both over 120 years old. They spoke with him telepathically about advanced hospitals and technology in the Galaxies.

William requested the help of two detectives, Pratt & Ratts, known to be the best. They agreed to investigate Lily Alberton's disappearance. Payment, as always, was not money but fruit and vegetables, which their spaceship processed into powders for medicine. Since the ship was invisible through electromagnetic fields, no one on Earth could see it.

Later, Lorena called William. "Remember to be home this weekend. It's Nolan's sixteenth birthday."
"Yes, Mom. I love him like a brother. Please go to BBC Couture and order a suit for him, tailored to his size. Pick it up Saturday morning. This way it will be a surprise."
"That's a good idea, son."
"Mom, don't worry about the cost. A man I helped this week gave me a gift of seven hundred pounds."
"What's his name?"
"Mr. Carlos II Alberton."
Lorena gasped. "Do you realize who he is? One of the richest men in France! William, how did you meet him? Such people rarely speak to strangers."
"Just a coincidence, Mom."

That weekend, the family celebrated Nolan's birthday. He surprised William with a framed painting of his high school graduation picture. William hugged him. "You're the brother I always needed."

Dr. Carlos, Lorena's husband, added, "You and Nolan complete our family. I missed having a son, but now I do."
Aunt Emma smiled proudly. "This boy is a blessing."
Lorena embraced William and Nolan. "For years, I had only one son. Now God has given me a husband and another son."

Applause filled the room.

The next day, Lorena received a call from Mrs. Roberts. Crying, she said, "My husband passed away in the hospital today." William's grandfather had died, his weak heart unable to wait for a transplant.

Lorena told William, who immediately prepared to travel. Dr. Carlos arranged their trip for the funeral. Three days later, the whole family gathered. Afterward, they all returned home, and William went back to college.

Soon after, Lorena's mother, Evelyn, fell ill with asthma. She spent three days in the hospital, and Lorena stayed in Dijon overnight to be near her, going straight to work the next morning.

Three Months Later

Three months after William's grandfather passed away, he received a letter in the mail from his grandfather's home. It was part of the Testament. In it, William was left his grandfather's car and some money to help with college. During his time off from college, William went back to Manchester. He brought the car to a shop, where they repaired the engine, repainted it, and fitted new tires, making it look almost new again. It was a 1950 Ford.

Now, with only one more year left in college, William finally had transportation. He was set to graduate in November 1965.

One afternoon, Nolan came to William's room to chat. He said:

"In school, they were talking about the news from the mountains near Mount Everest. Some climbers said they saw a bright light in the sky, moving as fast as lightning.

The professor told us it might be visitors from other planets. He even said maybe from Mars—and that those creatures could be green and not like humans. What do you think, William?"

William smiled at his younger brother. "Well, Nolan, here on Earth, people don't know much about such things. Do you know why? Because governments don't want to spend much money on space research, even though astrologers say there are countless planets beyond our Earth. Some galaxies surely have life—maybe even civilizations more advanced than ours."

Nolan leaned forward. "So, you really think it's true?"

"That's my opinion," William said, choosing his words carefully. He was trying to open Nolan's eyes, but couldn't reveal the full truth about the galaxies. "As for green creatures, I don't believe that. They are probably just like us—though maybe they can take on different forms. One day, I'm sure scientists will investigate properly."

Nolan nodded thoughtfully. William then checked the clock. "Well, little brother, I need to catch the four o'clock train. I'll be back at college by six. Next week, when my car is ready, you and I will take it out for a short ride."

"That sounds great!" Nolan said with a smile. "See you, brother."

Lorena's Mother

Around the same time, Lorena's mother suffered a small infarct, which left her right side weakened. Lorena traveled to Dijon again to care for her. Emma Louis told her niece:

"She will need someone to help her daily."

Lorena replied, "I'll take her home until she requires professional nursing. I can arrange for a nurse to attend to her during my work hours, because it's hard to find someone trustworthy otherwise. Don't worry, Aunt Emma."

Her mother stayed in Lorena's home for about two months. Then she told Lorena she wanted to return to her sister Emma's house. "I feel happier there," she said, "because Emma is alone and I can keep her company. Here, you and your husband are busy with work, William is in college, Nolan is in school, and even though the nurse comes for three hours, I spend much of the day alone in this big house."

So Lorena took her mother back to her sister's, where both women were happy.

A Call from William

One evening, Lorena received a phone call from William.

"Hello, Mom."

"Hi, son. How are you? Something wrong? You never call me on Tuesdays."

"I know, Mom. Sorry. Today I spoke with Mr. Carlos II Alberton. He told me he would like you, Dad, and Nolan to join him at his hotel, the Plaza Square in Strasbourg. It's for his birthday and also the inauguration of his new club next to the hotel."

Lorena gasped. "That's the hotel for the rich! William, do we need tuxedos or gala suits?"

"Yes," William said. "That's what he told me. Mom, please talk to Dad and call me back. He also asked me to let you know that a limousine will come to pick you up. By the way, Aunt Emma will receive an invitation by mail, too."

"Oh my," Lorena said softly. "Our neighbors will think we are rich! William, that man must truly appreciate you."

"He does, Mom. He even offered to open a medical office for me in the Plaza once I graduate. He says he wants to adopt me as a son."

Lorena shook her head in amazement. "All right, son. I'll talk to your father and call you back. Goodnight."

"Goodnight, Mom."

Preparations

After hanging up, Lorena went to her husband's office.

"Carlos," she said, "William called."

"Something wrong?"

"No. But you know Mr. Carlos II Alberton, the millionaire?"

"Yes, what about him?"

"He invited us to his new club. William already has the invitation and said the limousine will pick us up. But we'll need tuxedos."

Dr. Carlos nodded. "These kinds of events are very exclusive. Not everyone is allowed in. But since William has the invitation, we should accept."

Later, Lorena called William back.

"Yes, Mom?"

"We'll attend. But what about the tuxedos?"

"Don't worry," William replied. "I gave the tailor your number. He'll come to the house to take Dad's and Nolan's measurements, and your dress size, too. Everything will be delivered one day before the event. Mr. Alberton insisted."

"All right, my son. I'll make the arrangements. Thank you."

The Investigation

Meanwhile, Pratt and Ratts continued their investigation into the disappearance of Mr. Carlos II Alberton's niece, Lily.

Using advanced Galactic methods, they traced back the events of that tragic night. Lily had been lured into the mountains by her secret boyfriend, Prince Phillis of Spain. He raped her, and in her desperation, she fled. But she stumbled, fell into a hidden cave, and broke her neck. Phillis buried her there, marking the spot with a crude cross, then returned to the castle as if nothing had happened.

William translated the detectives' report from Galactic script into English and prepared it for Mr. Carlos II. Two days later, he sent a letter to Jack Alberton, Carlos's son.

Three days later, William received a reply from Mr. Carlos II. In his letter, Carlos wrote:

"What should I do now? Your friends, the detectives, do not want to speak to the police. Should I report this? What do you advise?"

William replied:

"Yes, go to the police. Tell them you received an anonymous call with the location. Give them the map, mark the exact place, and mention that you suspect Prince Phillis. Leave it at that."

After reading William's advice, Carlos sat in silence, remembering. The last time he had seen Prince Phillis was with his sister. Two days later, his niece had vanished.

He decided to act. But instead of going directly to the authorities, he first hired a private detective, Lucio Ranger.

"Lucio," Carlos said, "I need you to find my niece's body. Rent a four-wheel-drive truck, at least for a week. The area is high in the mountains."

Lucio asked, "Are you sure?"

"Yes. Whatever it takes, Lucio. I want her found. The cost does not matter."

Lucio agreed. "I'll go tomorrow."

And the search began.

William was speaking with Tarsi, the head of security in the Galaxies, about the money situation. William explained that he didn't want anything in return, but Tarsi insisted, "It's your money. You've been so good to us." William replied, "Next week, bring me a space capsule. I have lots of things to send home. Thank you." He also requested, "Send me pictures of Pratt and Ratts, the detectives, but make them look like Earth people, not in their Galaxy suits." Tarsi assured him, "Not a problem. You'll have them tonight."

Two days later, William received the pictures. He called Mr. Carlos II Alberton and told him, "I'll send you the photos of the two detectives handling your niece's case. This is just for you to know who they are—do not tell anyone. They do international work in many countries." Mr. Carlos replied, "Fine, William. As long as they did their job well and found my niece's body, that's what matters to me. And don't forget, next weekend we have the big party. I got your note, and I'm glad your mother, father, and brother will be there. Tell them to call the limousine— you have the number—so they can be picked up at the time they prefer." William agreed, "Yes, I'll explain everything to them."

Meanwhile, Camila had just finished her high school graduation and decided to go to a community college. She planned to study accounting because she would eventually take over her father's company. However, she broke up with William after listening to her mother, who insisted that William was too busy and didn't have time for her. Her mother also encouraged her to be with Adam Luckman, a boy who lived nearby. Adam's father was a lawyer with a large firm, and Adam often spent time with Camila, taking her out and giving her attention.

Camila's mother told her, "William is always occupied with school. You need a man who will take care of you." William had told Camila earlier that he wanted to finish medical college first, and if she could wait, they could stay together. But Camila chose to end the relationship.

When William mentioned this to his mother, Lorena, she said, "I'm sorry to hear that." William responded, "It's okay, Mom. After I become a doctor, I'll have time for any girl. Honestly, if I had to see her every time I came home or went to her house, I wouldn't have time for my studies. She doesn't understand how hard medical school is."

Lorena's sister, Emma, was visiting and overheard. She told William, "Well, you do whatever has to be done to finish medical school. Don't let anything interrupt your studies." William smiled and replied, "Aunt Emma, you can bet on that."

A few days later, after William had sent supplies to the Galaxies, he received an urgent message. A rain of meteor fragments had struck, something that happened once every ten years. The meteors brought strong winds mixed with sand, and although the Galaxies had defense systems, when they happened suddenly, it was difficult to activate them in time. Many people were wounded.

William began traveling two nights a week to help, returning to Earth in the mornings so he could still attend college. At school, one of the Galaxy spacemen took notes on William's homework and stayed in his room. If anyone saw him, they believed it was William. This way, William's absence went unnoticed.

In Krypton, one of the Galaxy's largest cities, the hospital was filled with wounded people. Thanks to advanced technology, doctors never directly touch patients. Instead, they were placed on special medical beds inside a treatment room. Patients were connected to diagnostic suits, and computers analyzed their entire condition. If surgery was needed, doctors operated remotely from an adjoining room using robotic arms with precision instruments.

The process was fast—after surgery, the same bed transported the patient to recovery in a protective overhead case. William served as an operating doctor there. For regular illnesses, they also had a more mysterious treatment method using "main energy," but it was difficult and took much longer. Doctors had to attend a special energy school to learn it.

Chapter 8: The Quiet Miracle

William's stepfather's mother, Mrs. Lilian Phillis, became very sick and was taken to the hospital. She suffered from severe stomach pain. Her son, Doctor Carlos, suspected appendicitis, but since he was not a surgeon, his colleague and friend, Dr. Robert Douglas, was called to operate.

When William came home, he went to see her. He always called her "Grandma." At the hospital, he asked if he could pray for her in private. His mother told her husband, "Let William go in with her. Let him pray. I have faith in my son; she will feel better."

While the rest of the family waited in the cafeteria, William held his grandmother's hand and whispered, "Grandma, you will feel better." He gently checked her stomach, gave her a small dose of medicine with some water, and let her rest. She didn't realize what he had done, but soon she fell asleep peacefully.

William left the room and joined the family in the cafeteria. His stepfather asked, "How is she now?" William replied, "She's sleeping. She was in terrible pain, so I gave her something mild to help. At home, the pills weren't working. Honestly, I think she should have been operated on immediately when we arrived at the hospital. But Dr. Robert said he has already ordered medicine to keep her relaxed tonight."

Later, when the family returned to her room, they found her still in a deep sleep. Dr. Carlos turned to Lorena and said, "I admire your strong faith in our son William. He reminds me of one of my neighbors he helped before. I am a doctor, but I've never seen anything like this. He seems to have a connection with God—or something. To be honest, yesterday I thought Mother might die. She screamed in pain at home, and now, suddenly, she is resting so peacefully. Your son has a special talent. I noticed it when he was in high school. He finished two years of school in one. While in sixth grade, he took some seventh- and eighth-grade classes ahead of time. And I've heard he has healed a few people with his prayers."

Naturally, Mrs. Lorena did not know that William was already a doctor in the Galaxies. She simply believed he had angels watching over him.

The surprise came the next morning—Mrs. Lilian woke up feeling much better. The nurses said she had slept peacefully through the night, and Dr. Robert found no alarming problems. After running an ultrasound, he told Dr. Carlos, "There's just some slight inflammation. I'll prescribe her medicine and send her home. If no more pain returns, she will be fine."

Mrs. Lilian smiled and said to her son, "Carlos, I feel wonderful. No pain at all." Dr. Robert nodded and said, "See? I told you, Carlos. Sometimes things heal better than expected."

But Dr. Carlos couldn't stop thinking. He quietly wondered if William had performed a miracle on his mother.

Back at college, William received a phone call from Strasbourg's Second Division Police. "This is Detective Colton," the man said. "We've located the body of the young girl who disappeared four years ago."

"That is very good news," William replied. "I'm sure Mr. Carlos II Alberton will be relieved."

"He is," the detective confirmed. "And I know you don't want your detectives revealed, but I was hoping to meet them. They are due to receive the *Detective of the Year* award, plus two thousand pounds in prize money. The only issue is, I don't know when they will contact me again. If you hear from them, please let me know. By the way, we already found evidence against Prince Phillis. Interpol is handling the case now. He'll be in France for at least a month."

Later, after the autopsy, Mr. Carlos II Alberton finally received his niece's body. Together with her parents, John and Mrs. Alberton, they held a funeral, and one week later, the burial took place.

That same week, a grand party was held at the new club. A limousine picked up William's family and brought them to the event. At the entrance, they were greeted by Mr. Carlos II and his son Jack, who escorted them to their reserved table. William sat proudly with his family.

Before the show began, Mr. Carlos II stood at their table and said to the guests:

"Your boy saved my life. Not only that, he and his detectives helped solve the case of my niece, who had been missing for four years. If you don't mind, I treat him as if he were my own grandson."

Mrs. Lorena smiled and said, "This is my son, and he is always ready to help anyone in need."

Doctor Carlos added, "I love him as much as I love my other son, Nolan. He is truly a remarkable young man."

Mr. Carlos II Alberton went further: "After William graduates from medical school, I have a building two blocks from here. I will renovate it and give him the first floor for his own medical practice. I know he will be an excellent doctor. I've already spoken to my old physician about him. Just one medicine he prescribed for me proved that William has extraordinary knowledge. That's why I believe we have the best doctor in our family already."

William smiled humbly and said, "Dad, I'll always be the same person—helping anyone who needs it."

"I know that, son," replied Dr. Carlos.

The show began, filled with music and performances, and the family enjoyed themselves greatly. Mrs. Lorena leaned toward her husband and whispered, "This is the first time I've ever been to a party with such wealthy people. It's an experience I'll never forget."

One afternoon, William received a surprise letter in the mail. He had always known, from his grandmother, Mrs. Elizabeth, that he had two aunts—his father's sisters—but he never had much contact with them. Both were professionals: Olivia was a nurse, married to a doctor, and living in Scotland with two sons; Rossi was a dentist, living in Frankfurt, Germany, married to a German Air Force officer, and with one daughter.

It was Rossi who had written the letter. William had briefly seen her at his grandfather's funeral, but they hadn't had time to talk because he had left for his grandmother's house. In her letter, Rossi explained:

"I had hoped to meet you when you visited your mother's house, but I was told you had already gone back to medical school. However, I will be in your town soon. I have a dental convention scheduled from November 10th to the 15th—just ten days from now. If you have time, please let me know. I'll be staying at the hotel across the street from the Convention Center. I also plan to see your mother, Lorena. My dear nephew, I will see you soon."

William was delighted with the letter. He had always wanted to know his aunts better. His mother also encouraged him, saying, "Olivia is also interested in meeting you someday. Both of your father's sisters were wonderful students. When I married your father, Rossi was always smiling, while Olivia was more reserved, much like your grandfather. You'll see—they are remarkable women."

William decided to write back immediately, asking Rossi to come to their house after her convention. "Is that okay, Mom?" he asked. His mother agreed.

Meanwhile, William continued his unusual work with the detectives from the Galaxies. These were not ordinary men, but beings from beyond Earth—between the regions near Jupiter—who many on Earth didn't even believe existed. William had first met them in a Krypton hospital, where they were guarding two criminals who had broken intergalactic laws. They were relentless in enforcing justice.

To appear in Strasbourg, they disguised themselves as earthly detectives, impersonating others who had died in different countries. They had the power to make everyone believe they were real. Even when police captains called foreign stations to confirm, they received the answer that these men were indeed active detectives. Nobody suspected the truth: they were outer-space agents.

At the Strasbourg Police Meeting, they received an award and a check for two thousand pounds as *Detectives of the Year*. Later, they stopped by William's medical school and gave him the check, explaining, "This money is no use to us. In our system, all transactions are electronic, like advanced credit cards. But we are waiting for the fruit and supplies you prepare for us—we can take those back home."

When Rossi finally arrived for her convention in Paris, everything went as planned. William went to her hotel to meet her. She was overjoyed to see her nephew.

"My dear boy," she said warmly, "so many years have passed since I last saw Lorena. Look at you—you're so tall now. I remember a picture of you and your mother at Grandma's house, taken at Christmas when you were about eight years old. You look exactly like your father. My mother always said so. The only difference is—you're even smarter. I read about you in the German newspapers when the governor awarded you that scholarship for medical school. I showed my husband Gerald and told him proudly, 'This is my nephew!'"

She went on, "I have a daughter, Lucy. She's in college as well. On Friday, once the convention is over, I plan to visit your mother. If you'd like, you could come with me."

William explained, "My stepfather, Carlos, said he would pick us up on Friday evening. I have work to finish at the college in the Dean's office during the morning, but I'll be free for the weekend."

"That's wonderful," Rossi smiled. "I'll call my husband to let him know I'll be spending the weekend with my ex-sister-in-law. Gray's mother and my mother will be so happy. Now, William, would you like to have dinner with me tonight?"

"Yes, Aunt, I'm hungry too," William said.

"Then let's go to the dining room. But first, I'll call your stepfather so he knows about Friday's plans," Rossi said.

They enjoyed dinner together, and afterward, William said, "It's time for me to go home, Aunt. I'll see you on Friday evening."

"Goodbye, William. Say hello to your mother for me. Here's the hotel number—tell her to call me."

"I will, Aunt. See you soon."

Back at home, William found his stepbrother, Nolan, injured after a soccer game. Nolan was lying down with ice on his right knee. Dr. Carlos said it was probably just a muscle strain.

William checked him carefully. "Brother, what I'm about to do may hurt a little, but afterward you'll feel much better. I treated a football player with the same problem last week."

Dr. Carlos nodded knowingly. "I have an idea of what you're planning. Nolan is in pain now, son, but later he'll be okay. At the hospital, they would only give massages— it would take much longer. Do what you can for him."

William asked his father to remove the ice. Then he went downstairs to speak with his mother, Lorena, explaining that Nolan was in pain, but he would take care of it. Lorena said, "I trust William. If he says he can help, let him."

Half an hour later, William returned to Nolan's room. "This will hurt, I know," he said gently. Then he touched his brother's head and began counting softly to twenty. Nolan drifted into a deep sleep.

With the help of a nurse who appeared with special instruments, William treated Nolan's knee. He cleaned and repaired the torn meniscus using advanced tools from the Galaxies. After wrapping the leg with gauze, the nurse disappeared.

When Nolan awoke, he said, "I had a dream—I saw a nurse with you, operating on my leg in the hospital. But I feel much better now, just a little sore."

"Don't walk too much tomorrow," William advised. "Use crutches for two days, and then you'll be fine."

Dr. Carlos and Lorena entered the room and were amazed to see Nolan's leg wrapped professionally.

"William," Dr. Carlos said, astonished, "you're already a doctor. Did you operate on him?"

William shook his head. "Not exactly. I just treated the muscle."

But in truth, he had performed a delicate operation with the advanced techniques he had learned in the Galaxies.

The next day was Friday. William left for college to finish his work at the Dean's office. Before leaving, he left a note for his stepfather reminding him to pick up Aunt Rossi in the evening.

The next morning, Nolan came downstairs to the first floor. His father, Dr. Carlos, and Lorena were in the kitchen preparing breakfast. Dr. Carlos soon moved into the living room to read the newspaper.

Lorena asked Nolan, "How do you feel?"

"Mom, I feel fine—just a little sore when I put weight on my leg," Nolan replied.

"What did your brother tell you?" Lorena asked.

"He told me to use the crutches," Nolan admitted, "but I didn't."

Dr. Carlos overheard and walked back into the kitchen. "Where are the crutches, Nolan?"

"In my room, Dad."

"Alright," Dr. Carlos said, "I'll go get them for you so you can use them."

"Thank you, Dad," Nolan replied.

Dr. Carlos sat down at the table as Lorena served him a cup of black coffee. He looked thoughtful. "Lorena," he said, "William is already a doctor. The way he treated Nolan yesterday was as if he were in a hospital. He is our son, but to me, he feels almost supernatural. He knows exactly what his patients need, even without equipment. It's like magic."

Lorena smiled. "That's William. I believe he's had this gift since high school. Do you remember when we were renting the house downtown? One evening, Sarah, our neighbor, came knocking on the door. William answered. She asked if I was home yet. He told her I would be home soon from work and asked why. She explained her father was having an asthma attack and asked if we had any remedies. William told her, 'Let's go see him. I'll pray for him until my mother comes.'

"He went with her, took some cold tablets, and asked everyone to let him be alone with the sick man. When I got home, I found a note from William and went straight to Sarah's house. To my surprise, I found Sarah, her father Peter—he was about seventy-five—and my son together. Sarah said, 'Lorena, thank God your son was here. He prayed for my father, and now his breathing is normal. He hasn't even used his inhaler.'

"Two days later, reporters came asking to write about it. I told them I wouldn't allow William to be left alone with their questions. But three days later, I read the newspapers, and there it was."

Dr. Carlos took a sip of his coffee and nodded. "Sweetheart, do you realize what this means? We have a special son. His talent is something neither you nor I nor anyone else has. I believe God guides him. He will become Dr. William Roberts, one of the greatest doctors of all time. Laboratories will compete for him. He will be rich and respected, and his scientific discoveries will change the world."

Lorena said softly, "Yes, but William is so humble. His talent won't change who he is."

Dr. Carlos glanced at the clock. "Honey, it's already three o'clock. We need to leave for the Convention Center. Nolan wants to come too—he says he feels better. Tell him to hurry, or we'll be late."

Nolan came down from his room. "I'm ready, Dad."

"Alright, let's go. See you later, Mom," Dr. Carlos said.

"Goodbye, sweetheart," Lorena replied, and they left.

About an hour later, they arrived at the **Hotel Eiffel** in Paris. William was waiting across the street. He walked over to the car as they pulled up. At the hotel entrance, a bellman asked, "May I help you, sir?"

"Yes," Dr. Carlos said, "we're meeting Dr. Rossi Roberts."

"Of course," the bellman replied, guiding them into the reception room. He spoke to the front desk, who phoned Rossi. Ten minutes later, she appeared.

William stood up. "Aunt Rossi, this is my father, Dr. Carlos, and my brother, Nolan."

Rossi smiled warmly and shook their hands. "It's a pleasure to meet you all. I would love to have dinner with you today—William, Nolan, and Dr. Carlos. What do you say?"

Dr. Carlos glanced at his watch. "It's already five o'clock. If we leave now, we'll be home by six-thirty. Lorena has prepared a big dinner for you—she told me it would be a surprise."

"Very well," Rossi said. "Let me check out and bring my suitcase."

The bellman helped her carry it to the car. Rossi thanked him with a tip, and soon they were on the road.

Inside the car, Dr. Carlos asked, "So, you live in Germany now? How did that come about?"

Rossi explained, "After the war, everything changed. I met my husband, Major Gerard Puffier, while he was studying psychology at college. The army paid for his studies. At the same time, I was in dental school. We married, both graduated, and moved to Germany. He became an army psychologist, and I worked as a dentist in a military hospital. Later, I joined a large dental practice in Frankfurt, where I've been ever since."

"What about your daughter?" William asked.

"She's in her third year of medical school at Frankfurt University. And yes, she speaks English and French fluently. She was the top student of her high school, winning honors as Student of the Year."

Rossi smiled. "Dr. Carlos, I'd like to invite your whole family to my home in Germany."

"That's a wonderful idea," Carlos said. "But we'll need to talk with Lorena about it."

"Yes," Rossi said, "we were such good friends years ago. I used to stop by her house every day after school. I missed her so much when she moved to South America."

By then, they had arrived at Carlos's home. Lorena was in the kitchen but came running when she heard voices in the garage. She pulled off her apron and opened the door.

"Rossi!" she cried. "I can't believe it's you. You look taller than the last time I saw you. How is your mother?"

"She's well," Rossi said. "But please, don't keep us standing here—let's go inside."

They entered, and Rossi admired the house. "Lorena, this is beautiful."

Carlos called for Marie, the housekeeper, to prepare dinner. As they waited, Rossi teased Lorena: "You haven't changed much—except your hair. It used to be jet black!"

Lorena laughed. "Yes, the gray has been covered with color. Time changes us all."

Soon, Marie announced that dinner was ready. Everyone gathered at the table.

"Lorena," Rossi asked, "is this roast beef the same one you used to make when I was young?"

"Yes," Lorena smiled. "That was William's surprise for you." Tears welled in Rossi's eyes as she remembered. "I still recall that Christmas when my brother brought the whole family to your house."

Later, Lorena asked, "Tell me more about your family."

"My husband Gerald is a wonderful man, an army psychologist. We have one daughter, Rossi Mary. She's in her third year of university and wants to be a lawyer— though we'll see if she changes her mind."

Lorena replied, "It would be a pleasure to visit you in Germany someday."

"Can you say yes, please?" Rossi urged.

"Alright," Lorena smiled. "We'll plan and let you know when to take our vacation."

Just then, the doorbell rang. Lorena told Rossi, "Now comes your surprise." She opened the door, and in walked **Olivia**, Rossi's sister.

The two sisters embraced, tears streaming down their faces. They hadn't seen each other in more than five years. With Olivia came Mrs. Emma Louis and Evelyn, Lorena's mother.

Rossi was amazed. "This is my aunt, Emma Louis? And my mother, Evelyn? I don't remember her well."

Evelyn explained gently, "That's because after I married your brother, we moved away with my father for his work. But we are family."

Everyone came inside from the chilly air. Olivia and Lorena sat together, and Lorena asked about her family.

"My husband is Dr. Richard Towson, head of the ER where I work," Olivia explained. "We have two sons. The older will graduate from university next year—he wants to be a doctor. In fact, he read the news in Scotland about William with the Governor. It was in the national papers. Lorena, you must be so proud."

"Yes," Lorena said with a smile. "In one more year, William will finish medical school and begin his internship. We don't yet know where, but his future is bright."

Chapter 9: Shadows of Love and Duty

After that week of family reunion and good times, William returned to college. The following week was full of work—Botany and Pharmacy studies that involved countless books to read. No matter what, the work was demanding.

At the same time, in the Galaxies, an epidemic broke out. It resembled a yellow fever-like illness on Earth, though they had a different name for it. Fortunately, they already had remedies and a vaccine. William's clone was called almost every night to help, and in one colony, several lives had already been lost.

William had a very good doctor friend in the Galaxy Hospital named **Tatty N5**, whose medical license ID. She had blond hair, blue eyes, and a graceful figure. William believed she could become his girlfriend in the future, after he finished medical college and became a doctor. The only problem was that he would need to live in the Galaxy—she could not survive on Earth for long. To stay, she would need to take on a different body each time she wished to appear. William knew a strong decision lay ahead of him, but he was daunted by it.

One of his close galaxy friends asked if he had thought seriously about it. The situation between William and Tatty was sad—it seemed as though she would always be there in the Galaxies, while William remained on Earth. At some point, it bothered her deeply, for a woman's unhappiness was unlike anything else. All the other girls in the Galaxies seemed happy, except her. One of William's friends had been observing them for two years and commented:

"I know this is hard, William. But I've been watching you two for a long time. This will not lead you to a place where

the weight of the world can be defied. All I can do is watch you fall. It feels like a foolish dream."

William, sitting in the doctor's room, lifted a glass of water, took a sip, then shifted from one leg to the other. But he did not respond. Instead, he changed the subject and left for Earth.

Meanwhile, on Earth, Lorena's neighbor Violet came by. She rang the doorbell, and Lorena opened it.

"Hi, Violet, how are you?" Lorena asked.

"I'm going crazy," Violet replied.

"Why?"

"My two daughters argue about everything. Can you come have a cup of coffee at my house? I need to talk."

Lorena agreed, excused herself to the bathroom quickly, and then joined her. They walked to Violet's home, where the two daughters were indeed arguing. Violet called out to them. Lori explained that she had found letters on top of her sister Susan's bureau, which started the argument.

When Violet called Susan to come downstairs, she refused at first. But five minutes later, Susan's boyfriend Felipe knocked at the door. Violet let him in, and Susan rushed down after hearing his voice. She quickly fixed her hair before greeting him, and they began talking in the living room.

Meanwhile, Violet and Lorena sat in the kitchen over coffee. Felipe complimented Susan's red dress, caressed her cheek, and spoke sweetly about the time they had shared at the party. Susan, only sixteen, seemed deeply taken by him, which worried Violet.

"There's nothing I can do," Violet confessed to Lorena. "She's only sixteen."

"What does her father say?" Lorena asked.

"The problem is—he doesn't say anything at all," Violet replied with frustration.

They spoke a little longer about Susan's behavior and possible problems at school, but finally Lorena excused herself. "Thank you for the coffee, Violet. I need to finish the laundry. Tomorrow is a workday." Lorena was kind and always willing to help others, but with personal family issues like this, she often felt powerless.

That same week, Rossi and Olivia kept in touch with Lorena. Olivia called and invited her to a birthday party on **July 30th**, saying summer was almost over. Lorena hesitated:

"I can't answer right now, Olivia. I need to talk to my husband and William. I know he'll say it's fine. God is my witness, I never knew such good men existed. But the weather has been bad—strong winds and rain. That's what I heard at the hospital. I'll call you back. We'll need the whole weekend for your party. It's on Saturday, so we'd travel Friday afternoon, check into a hotel, and the next day leave from there for your home. But if the weather is bad, the train could be delayed."

Olivia reassured her, saying the strong winds were further south, and even invited Lorena and her family to stay at her house. Lorena thanked her and promised to pray for better weather. "I'll call you in two days," she added.

Meanwhile, William was very busy. The Galaxies were at war. One of the dominant galaxies had been destroyed twice. The governor there was cruel, and countless people had been killed, along with major buildings destroyed.

William's galaxy remained well protected, but casualties were still heavy after enemies broke into their system by cracking the entry code. Though they managed to repel the attack, the **Black Eye Galaxies**—their fiercest enemies—continued to regroup.

Because of this, William spent much of his time visiting hospitals in the Galaxies, while also struggling with his medical school schedule on Earth. His clone, Runts, had to cover for him. But Runts fell ill, missing two classes. William, sensing it through their connection, touched his mouth and realized something was wrong. He left the Galaxies to attend medical school himself.

Runts, though very intelligent and destined to be a doctor in his own galaxy, apologized for failing. William placed his hand on Runts' shoulder in reassurance. But before they could discuss it further, their main communication was suddenly interrupted.

Mr. Carlos II Alberton sent an invitation for William to visit him at his hotel. William returned to the same hotel where the party had once been held. Mr. Carlos II was delighted to see him, though he was a little sick with a cold brought on by the change in weather.

"Let me check you," William said.

"I'm okay, it's probably just a cold," replied Mr. Carlos.

William examined his lungs. "Did you have a fever?"

"Yes, last night. My wife gave me some home remedies, and I felt a little better."

"Well, Mr. Carlos," William said gently, "I'll send your driver to the pharmacy to get this medicine. If you don't feel better, go to the hospital as soon as possible. This is more than a simple cold—you're close to pneumonia."

William applied a medicinal ointment to his back and reminded him again that he needed proper treatment.

But Mr. Carlos shook his head. "The reason I asked you here today isn't just because I'm sick. I want to go to my son's house with you. He and I have a big surprise for you."

"Okay, Mr. Carlos, but not today," William insisted. "You're sick and need to rest. When John, your driver, returns, let him take you home. No meetings today—it will only make things worse. What you need is rest."

Mr. Carlos cupped his hands around his mouth. "Not today, William! I do have a meeting in about an hour. Don't call him Mr. Jack—he's my son. And you are not just a guest— you're my grandson. I never had one before. Call my son Jack."

William smiled. "Okay, Grandpapa. I like that. I love you."

"I love you too, my boy," Carlos said, his voice softening. He called Jack, and William suggested they go to the dining room. As they stepped out of the office, Jack came running.

"Dad, are you okay?" Jack's voice trembled.

"Calm down, son. I'm okay," Carlos reassured him.

William explained that his father needed at least one week of rest. Jack's eyes widened with concern. "Oh no… but if he rests, he'll be fine?"

"Yes," William said, "with medicine and rest, he'll recover."

Carlos smiled proudly. "Did you hear that, son? He is my grandson."

"I know, Daddy," Jack replied, hugging William.

"Let's go home," Jack said.

They waited for the medication William prescribed. Jack phoned the pharmacy, and within ten minutes, John the driver returned with it.

"John," Carlos said, "this is my grandson. Make sure everyone here treats him with the same respect as me."

"Yes, sir," John said with a smile. "It's a pleasure to meet you, William."

"Just call me William," he replied warmly.

After some time, Jack invited William to visit his mother's house. "One of the hotel limo drivers will take you home afterward," he said.

William agreed, and they all helped Mr. Carlos, who had dozed off in the car. When they arrived, Jack explained the neighborhood to William—it had once been farmland, about thirty acres, until a construction company proposed a new development. Now, the New Hoppe Community was a thriving area with forty houses, each worth at least three hundred thousand pounds.

At last, they reached the mansion—Jack's mother's home, a grand house with eight bedrooms and a driveway stretching one hundred and fifty meters.

Inside, Mrs. Ariana Alberton greeted them warmly. "William, I'm so glad you've come into our family. Jack talks about you constantly, as if you were his brother. I've never seen him speak of anyone with such affection."

She praised her husband of forty years as the best man she had ever known, though she admitted he never listened to doctors. "It's a miracle he listened to you," she said.

William smiled. "I told him the truth—that he's very sick, but if he rests and takes his medicine, he'll recover and be back to his business soon."

"That's because you're his adopted grandson," Carlos said proudly.

The room was filled with laughter and warmth. Roberta, the head maid, served coffee and desserts.

"How old are you, son?" Mrs. Ariana asked.

"Twenty," William answered.

"And already a doctor?"

Jack beamed. "Mom, I told you—he's the smartest student in medical school. The governor himself paid for his studies. He'll graduate next November, the 12th."

"Then you'll practice at the British RAMC Hospital," Mrs. Ariana said. "That is wonderful."

Jack nodded. "No one believes it because William is so humble."

"Thank you for your kind words," William said.

Mrs. Ariana offered, "Why don't you stay overnight? The guest room is ready."

William agreed. Later that night, though, he had to leave for the Galaxies. A battle had just ended, and many soldiers were injured. He returned to Earth at six in the morning, showered, and came downstairs.

Roberta greeted him. "Good morning, Mr. William. Coffee?"

"Yes, thank you," he replied. While waiting, he glanced at the newspaper. The front page reported that the Alberton family was the fourth richest in France.

Roberta asked shyly, "You're a doctor, right? My mother works at this hotel, but she has terrible pain in her right leg. After work, she can hardly do anything."

"Tell her I'll see her at the hotel on Monday," William assured her.

"Thank you, Mr. William!"

Later, Carlos and Ariana joined him for breakfast. Carlos announced, "My wife and I have decided—you'll be our family doctor. Until you graduate, we'll call you and send a driver to wherever you are. You'll be paid monthly as our official physician. And after graduation, you'll have your own office, and even our employees can rely on your services."

William was touched. "Grandpa, I don't know what to say…"

They were interrupted by Larson, Ariana's dog, who ran to William and lifted his paw. William bent down, looked into the dog's eyes, and somehow communicated with him, as he could with all animals.

Soon, breakfast was served. As they finished, Mr. Carlos told William, "Your parents called me. I would like to speak with them."

William promised he would arrange it. A limo was already waiting. Joseph, the driver, took him home.

When William stepped out, he found his mother, Lorena, and his brother Nolan waiting outside.

"Hi, Mom," William said cheerfully.

Nolan grinned. "You came in a limo?!"

"Yes," William smiled. "It belongs to the Albertons. They're very wealthy—one of the richest families in France."

His mother nodded. "William, you have some letters in your room. Do you want to eat first?"

"Later, Mom. How's Dad?"

"He's fine. He visited his parents on Friday. They were asking for you."

"What did you tell them?" William asked.

"That you were away visiting," Lorena said simply. Then she looked at him seriously. "Mr. Carlos II told me he wants to speak to me and your father. Do you know why?"

"No, Mom," William answered honestly. "But he said he wants me to be not only his doctor, but the doctor for the whole family."

Lorena shook her head. "But William, you're not a doctor yet. You need a license."

"I know. But next month, they'll give me a temporary license for hospital practice. That's why I don't need to work at the restaurant anymore—Mr. Carlos will pay me monthly. He and his wife see me as their adopted grandson."

Lorena sighed, half-worried, half-proud. "My son, that is wonderful… but be careful."

"What I am thinking," Lorena said, "is that they may want to talk to you about it. My son, I love you, but I do not always know what you do or make in college, or anywhere. I'm not fussing, but I do recommend you be careful with those people; they are multi-millionaires."

"Mom, don't worry. I'm okay. On the other hand, I don't want to be hurt if something goes wrong," William replied.

His mother never knew, at that time, that William could
read people's hearts as well as their words. He already
knew the Albertons truly loved him. She did not understand
that they were very honest whenever they spoke to him.

"William, next week is Olivia's party. Can you make it?"

"I think I'll be okay. We have some hospital classes for
another week, and I'll be practicing. Mom, next month is
December. This will be the second Christmas in this house.
After I finish Medical School on November 12, I'll have
enough time to decorate the house outside."

Nolan came into the kitchen just then, hearing about it.
"I'd like to do that so much. During the holidays in
December, my grandpa always spent a lot of time
decorating inside and outside the house. He taught me, so
I'll be your helper."

"That sounds good," Lorena replied. "Hold your horses,
boys. You and your dad can handle the electric part, and
you two do the decorations."

Nolan smiled. "William, I was waiting for you to come
home. I need your help, little brother. I'm so glad you're
here."

"Of course, I'll help you," William said. "But first, let me
see what mail I have in my room."

Later, in Nolan's room, his brother explained, "I need to
take the test to qualify for university. I want you to tell me
which parts of my books I should study more."

William nodded. "I'll make it easier for you. I'll create
some practice material like a university test. You answer it,

and then you'll know which points you need to study.
You'll pass if you focus."

"You're the best brother anyone could want," Nolan said.

"Not the best," William corrected gently. "You just have to
concentrate and study every point."

Nolan went on. "Last week, the geography teacher talked
about planets that rotate around the sun. He said some
scientists believe there is life on those planets, but if they
do exist, they probably live like Indians—making cabins
above the ground."

William smiled. "I've read some books about that. One
story was about a girl who claimed to have met someone
from outer space when she was small. They took her into a
flying saucer. For years, no one saw her, and now nobody
knows what happened to her. But the truth is, they have
strong cities, underground rivers instead of oceans, and
they fly normally instead of using cars. They have
sophisticated weapons, and the strongest defense is their
invisibility. Their hospitals are advanced, and they can even
cover a spaceship with a magnetic field so nobody can
attack. But they also have problems: freezing temperatures
for months, very short summers, and dangerous gravity.
That's why if we went there, we'd float in the air."

Nolan asked, "How long would it take to travel to those
galaxies?"

"Here on Earth, without supersonic spacecraft, it would
take more than two years. But the real problem is building
the ship. We don't have the technology or equipment. They
do. We are living in 1964, but in their world, it's like the
year 2025. Their cars fly, their public transport is

underground, and their subways are controlled with special technology. It's a different world."

"William," Nolan said, "I'll need help with algebra."

"Okay," William agreed. "Tonight, before bed."

Just then, Doctor Carlos, William's stepfather, came home. "Hi, son."

"Hi, Dad."

"I saw in the newspaper that your college selected you as *Student of the Year*. Congratulations."

"Thanks, Dad."

"Your mom knows, because I got the invitation for the ceremony on December 20, 1964. The prize is three thousand pounds, and the governor will add ten thousand more. Why didn't you tell your mother?"

"I was waiting," William admitted.

"You're the best kid anyone could want," his stepfather said, hugging him. "But don't say anything to your mother yet. I ordered new shoes for everyone. Oh—and they had a party for me at the Woolf Club. I was promoted to Head of Hospitals."

"Great, Dad. Congratulations!" William gave him a big hug.

Lorena entered. "Carlos, what are you two talking about?"

They quickly changed the subject, but later William told her the truth. "Mom, after dinner, I'll share something."

She smiled. "What is it?"

"Well, on December 20 at the college ceremony, I'll be named *Medical Student of the Year*."

"Yes, I know," she said, smiling. "Your father saw it in the newspaper. It's a big surprise. Nurses and doctors at the hospital already congratulated me. You're even in an international magazine. Your Aunt Rossi is so proud— you've reached a great title."

At Nolan's school, the director called him into the office. "The *Medical Student of the Year* in the newspaper—he's your brother?"

"Yes," Nolan said proudly.

"Well, then, you can follow in his footsteps, too. He must be a genius."

The next day, William read one of his letters. It was from a major laboratory in the U.K. They wanted him to visit, offering round-trip tickets and hotels, to discuss working in their scientific department.

William went downstairs to show his parents. "Mom, Dad, this letter is from the big laboratory in the U.K. They want me to work there."

Dr. Carlos nodded. "I knew this would happen soon. If you join them, you should also consider a scientific college. They'd pay for it."

William hesitated. "But Mr. Carlos Alberton offered me an office in downtown Strasbourg. He's rebuilding a building right now. It'll be ready by the time I graduate."

"Then," Dr. Carlos advised, "why not do both? Work in a U.K. hospital and laboratory for now, then later take your office. You'll be young enough to decide."

They phoned Mr. Alberton that evening.

"I'm so glad you called," Mr. Alberton said warmly. "William is like a grandson to me. My wife and I want to adopt him as our grandson officially. If you agree, we can arrange it with lawyers."

Lorena smiled. "He is twenty years old now. He is free to make his own decisions. But we appreciate your love for him."

Mr. Alberton went on: "He came to my office when I was sick and made me take a week of rest at home. His medicine and care saved me. Everyone in my family loves him. We want him as one of us."

After the call, William said softly, "They treat me like family. All the drivers know my address. They even send cars to the college if they need me. Grandpa Carlos Alberton says he wants me to be their family doctor once I graduate."

His stepfather put a hand on his shoulder. "Son, this is a good thing. They are multi-millionaires. If they adopt you as family, you'll be secure, and your office will be in the heart of downtown. But remember, become a heart specialist. That way, you'll attract even more important patients."

Later, William opened another letter. It was a wedding invitation—from Camila Locksheed. He frowned. The wedding was the same day as his college award ceremony. He remembered her boyfriend, a troubled young man, not yet mature, though from a well-known lawyer's family. William thought about it. He still felt something unresolved with her, but in his heart, he knew where he needed to be that day.

Chapter 10: The Grand Ceremony

Two weeks later, William finished his college classes for the holidays. Mr. Carlos II called and asked him to come to his house.

"Yes, what time should I be there?" William asked.

"About two o'clock today. The limo will pick you up at one," Mr. Carlos replied.

"Alright, see you later," said William.

Around the same time, his aunt Olivia had written him a letter. She wished to attend the Medical School ceremony and asked if she needed an invitation. William wrote back:

"Aunt, I will send you three invitations. I also spoke to my mother — if you'd like to stay at our house, you are welcome. I love you, Aunt Olivia. Best wishes to you and the rest of the family. Be well. Love, William."

That afternoon, William prepared for his visit. Coming down the stairway, he passed through the kitchen, where the service lady, Lucy, greeted him.

"Would you like something to eat, sir?" she asked.

"Yes, Lucy. Could you make me a chicken sandwich? I'll be in the living room," William replied.

"Of course," she said with a smile.

An hour later, the limousine arrived. The driver greeted him:

"Good afternoon, Mr. William. How are you, sir?"

"Fine, thank you."

"Mr. Carlos asked me to take you downtown first. He has a meeting with Japanese business partners, so we won't go to the house just yet."

"That's fine. Your name is Joseph, right?"

"Yes, sir."

Minutes later, the limo pulled into a large downtown building and parked in the garage.

"The stairway to the second floor is just on the right," Joseph said.

William thanked him and followed the stairs up. From outside the door, he could hear voices from inside the meeting. Jack, Mr. Carlos's son, came out to greet him.

"William! How are you?"

"I'm fine," William answered.

"Come, sit with me. My father's almost finished. Would you like some coffee?"

"Yes, thank you."

Jack showed him to the table. "The big day is only five days away," he said. "We're all ready to be there for you."

"Thank you, Jack," William replied warmly.

Soon after, the meeting ended. Mr. Carlos II entered the room, smiling broadly.

"Ah, my grandson, how are you today?"

"Very well, Grandpa," William replied.

They sat down together, Jack on one side, and three lawyers entered with briefcases.

"William," said Mr. Carlos, "these men are the company lawyers — Mr. Lauren Derty, John Smith, and Richard Ransom. They've prepared the documents for your adoption into our family. This will give you all the legal rights of our grandson. It's our wish — mine, my wife's, and Jack's. But it's your decision."

William stood, his voice steady. "It is a great privilege to be part of your family. But I want you to know, I have no interest in your wealth or possessions. From the first day we met, what mattered to me was the love and kindness you showed. I only want to belong to this family with love in my heart, nothing more."

Tears welled in Jack's eyes. Mr. Carlos rose and embraced William.

"That is why I love you," he said. "I know you are humble. But these papers make it official. With them, our accountant can handle expenses legally, like your transportation and salary. It's better this way."

The lawyers placed the documents on the table. Signatures were given — William's, Mr. Carlos's, and the witnesses'. Richard gathered the papers.

"These will be authenticated in court tomorrow. Copies will be sent to you, William."

"Perfect," Mr. Carlos said. "Thank you, Richard. Now, I must prepare for tomorrow's Japanese business contracts."

After the meeting, Mr. Carlos turned to William. "Come, my grandson. My wife and some family members are waiting for us at the house."

They left the building and entered the waiting car.

"Shall I stop for ice?" the driver asked.

"No need, it's already delivered," Mr. Carlos answered.

Jack added, "Caroline just called — she's on her way to the house as well."

When they arrived, the family was gathered at the Alberton home. Mr. Carlos's wife greeted them warmly, kissing her husband and taking his arm.

"My husband has just brought home our eldest grandson," she announced proudly. "Friends, family — this is William. We are so proud of him, the finest student in his Medical School."

She introduced him around the room before leading everyone into the dining room. Dinner was served.

Jack's wife and their twin daughters sat nearby. "How tall are you?" she asked William.

"Six foot two," he replied with a smile.

Mr. Carlos chuckled. "Yes, Maya, he is tall — and a fine-looking young man as well."

Among the guests was Alice Ross, nineteen years old, a beautiful girl with an intelligent gaze. She was immediately drawn to William. They spoke easily, both of them students, and their conversation carried on.

Alice's father, Mr. Jaxson Ross, an engineer who owned several downtown buildings, came out to greet them.

"Soon to be a doctor, eh?" he said, shaking William's hand.

"Yes, sir. Just six more months," William replied.

Mr. Ross nodded. "I designed the blueprints for your new office downtown. Six examination rooms, prime location. Expensive, but worth it. You'll need other doctors there in time. For now, know this: my family and I will be your patients."

"Thank you, sir. That means a lot."

As they spoke, Mr. Ross took some pills from a bottle. Alice noticed.

"Dad, another headache?"

"Yes, sweetheart," he said.

William asked gently, "How long have you had these headaches?"

"About a year. My doctor thinks it's sinus-related. He gave me a spray, but it doesn't help much."

"It might be something more serious. If you'd like, I can check you properly sometime," William offered.

Before the conversation could continue, Mr. Carlos called for William.

Inside, Mrs. Virginia Alberton presented him with a gift: a fine suit.

"You must wear this at your ceremony," she said.

William smiled, deeply touched. "I love it, Grandma. Thank you." He embraced her warmly.

The driver came into the house. Mr. Carlos II said, *"Put those suits in my car, John. And this is William's suit. Don't forget, when he gets home, take it out of the car. He doesn't need it right away."*
"Yes, boss," John replied.

The party was over. Among the family friends, William noticed a man he didn't recognize. He quickly realized the man was drunk. The house security personnel were speaking to him, trying to convince him to go home. He hadn't done anything wrong—only tried to fall asleep on the big sofa. Later, William found out he was his grandfather's brother-in-law, an alcoholic who had been in treatment for years.

William was ready to go home when Mr. Carlos II himself helped escort the man out, holding him by the shoulders. It was late, almost one in the morning, when the driver finally took William back home.

The next morning—Sunday—his family was getting ready for church at Saint Michel Catholic Church. William was

still upstairs when Nolan came knocking on his door.
"Are you going to church?" Nolan asked.
"Yes, I'll be down in two minutes."
"Okay, brother."

When William came downstairs, the family was already waiting. *"Mom, William's coming,"* Nolan said. Finally, everyone was ready, and Dr. Carlos announced, *"Well, let's go."*

They drove off, stopping in front of the church. As they got out of the car, two older women approached Lorena.
"Is this your son?" one asked.
"Yes, this is William and Nolan," Lorena replied.
"We saw him in the newspapers—he's a smart boy."

Lorena smiled politely but kept walking, knowing they were running late. Inside, the family found a pew, knelt to pray, and mass began. Afterward, the priest spoke:
"Please, everyone, pay attention. Today, in our church, we have a special student. He did all his high school here, and now he's in medical school. This is Mr. William Roberts."

William stood, and the entire congregation applauded. *"It is a privilege for our school,"* the priest continued, *"because he is the number one student among all colleges."*

One of the high school teachers, Mr. Rogers, came to greet him. *"Hello, William,"* he said warmly.

As they left the church, William turned to his mother.
"Mom, do you remember Marcos's Restaurant? We used to stop there every Sunday for breakfast."
"Yes, but it's far from here."
"Mom, it's only twenty minutes away."

Dr. Carlos overheard and said, *"Let's go there."*
Lorena hesitated. *"It's a very small place, Carlos. Isn't that the one you used to visit on your lunch break?"*
"Yes, but this is my family. I can be comfortable anywhere we go."

They arrived at the restaurant, sat at a table, and a middle-aged waitress approached.
"Can I help you?" she asked.
"I'd like the strawberry pancakes," William said.
"Four or six?"
"Six, please—they're big, but I prefer that."

Everyone else ordered their meals. After they were served, the owner himself came to the table. *"How do you like everything?"* he asked.
"Very good," Lorena answered.
The man looked closer. *"Wait a minute—I remember you. You used to come every Sunday with your mom. And you always ordered strawberry pancakes! Your name is William, right?"*
"Yes, sir," William replied with a smile.
"I saw your picture in the newspapers, but I can't believe I'm seeing you here in my restaurant."

When the bill came, William quickly picked it up. *"I'll pay."*
"Son, let me pay," Dr. Carlos offered.
"No, Dad, this is my treat."
"Do you need money, son?" Lorena asked.
"No, Mom, don't worry—I'm fine."

They left, driving past the old hospital where Lorena used to work. Nolan looked out the window in surprise. *"Mom, is that the hospital where you worked before?"*
"Yes, Nolan. It was a good place. The doctors and nurses

worked very hard. Summers were tough—no air conditioning, only fans, and we had to open the hallway windows."

"Wow, Mom."

"Yes, Nolan, it wasn't an easy job. That was right after the war ended. Sometimes we had to wait weeks for supplies. It wasn't easy, and sadly, we lost patients because of those delays." Dr. Carlos added quietly.

Meanwhile, William was receiving messages from the Galaxies. Now that he was out of medical school, he had more time. He traveled at night, performing surgeries for patients who needed them. Four days later, he received a call from Mr. Carlos II.

"Hello, Grandpa."

"Hello, son. If you have time, can you come to the office today?"

"Okay, Grandpa. I can, around two o'clock. I just have morning rounds. But also, Jaxson Ross spoke to me yesterday about his headaches. I told him I'd check him. His face looks swollen; I think he's hiding how much he's suffering."

"Yes, he told me about that. Please see him this afternoon at his office."

"I'll call him and confirm. Bye, Grandpa."

Later that day, William arrived at Mr. Ross's office. After examining him, he discovered a tumor on his forehead and offered treatment using his Galaxy techniques. The procedure was successful, and Mr. Ross recovered quickly.

That evening, the Ross family invited William to dinner. Alice Ross, Jaxson's beautiful nineteen-year-old daughter, greeted him warmly. Her father, still amazed by William's skill, said, *"You're the best doctor I've ever known. When*

*you open your office downtown, people will be lined up to
see you.”*

After dinner, William excused himself. Mr. Ross walked
him to his car. *“That Ford—what year is it?”*
*“1939. It was my grandfather’s. I had the engine repaired
and repainted, but it burns too much gasoline, so I often
park it outside.”*

The next day, William returned to remove Mr. Ross’s
bandages, and everything looked good. Together, they
walked to a nearby restaurant for coffee. There, Mr. Ross
phoned Mr. Carlos II, who soon joined them.

“Jaxson, are you trying to steal my grandson?” Carlos
joked. The three men laughed together over coffee.

 William was at home. His mother called from the kitchen,
“Dinner is ready.”
His younger brother Nolan walked in carrying a small box.
“William, I have a present for you.”

William opened it and smiled. *“A beautiful cufflink set—it
looks like gold.”*
Their father stepped into the kitchen and confirmed, *“Yes,
it is gold.”*

William hugged his brother. *“Thank you, Nolan. Guess
what—I’ll wear these tonight.”*
Everyone was glad he liked the gift.

William then said, *“Mom, I’ll take a shower and get ready.
Also, can you do me a favor? Ask John, the driver, to come
inside and eat something.”*
“Don’t worry, son. I’ll take care of it,” Lorena replied.

She sent Nolan outside to bring John in. Nolan called to him, *"John, come inside and have some dinner."*
"Thank you," John replied gratefully.

When John entered, Lorena greeted him warmly. *"Hi, John. I'm William's mother. Sit here, and if you need anything, Iris will help you."*
"Thank you, Mrs. Lorena."

Iris then asked John if he'd like to eat.
"Yes, I've worked all night. I'd appreciate it," he said.
"Come with me," Iris answered. She led him into a small room next to the kitchen, where she set a plate on the table.

By six in the evening, the family had eaten and were dressed, ready for the evening. After dinner, William checked on John.
"Did you eat?"
"Yes, sir, it was delicious," John answered.

"We'll need to leave by seven to beat the traffic to the college parking lot," John added.
"No problem," William said.

Half an hour later, everyone was ready. The family climbed into the limo. Lorena looked around in surprise. *"Is this a new limo?"*
"Yes, Mrs. Lorena," John said. *"On the right side, you'll find licorice, Coke, ice, and everything you need for a drink. This limo is prepared for a party."*

They arrived at the college, where John told William, *"I'll park in the limo parking lot. You need to walk from here."*
"Okay, John."

The family walked until they reached Spectrum Place. At the gate, William asked for the passes. Nolan had them, handed them to him, and William passed them to the guard. They entered.

Before the ceremony began, William saw his adopted grandparents seated inside and went to greet them. Soon after, the program started.

At eight o'clock, the ceremony opened with the national hymn. Everyone stood. Then the director, Mr. Dean Laen Josep, spoke:

"Tonight is one of the most special nights in the history of this college. First, we honor the group of doctors who graduate today. They will serve in hospitals for their practice, and some will begin their specialties. But tonight is also extraordinary. After twenty years, another student has surpassed all academic records. He is already a doctor in every sense, and next year will officially graduate. Faculty agree he has a super mind. His name is Mr. William Roberts."

The audience rose to their feet, applauding as William walked to the front, where the deans and professors waited. He received the honor, and the Governor of Strasbourg City awarded him ten thousand pounds, with a promise that his future specialty would also be funded.

Taking the microphone, William said:
"Thank you to all faculty members for making me who I am today. A special thanks to my mother, the number one person in my life, my stepfather, Dr. Carlos Phillis, and my younger brother Nolan. I also have two very special people in my life—my grandparents, Mr. Carlos II Alberton and his wife, Virginia. They trusted me, showed me love, and

made me feel I have two families now. Finally, I want to thank my friends who came tonight, even traveling from outside this country. Thank you, everyone."

Applause filled the hall. Then Dean Runny Walls spoke: *"This year has been special. Not only is William the number one student of the year, but he also invented a file-modification system that transformed our office records. Engineers plan to manufacture it commercially, and William has signed a contract, earning him fifteen percent of production profits. Tonight, the general manager of the company, Mr. Peter Hasson, is here."*

Mr. Hasson stepped forward. *"Ladies and gentlemen, Mr. William Roberts is not only the top student of the year, but he is also the inventor of a system now in great demand. Our company has produced machines that print and organize files automatically. Tonight, I present William with his first check—fifteen thousand pounds."*

The audience applauded again as William accepted the check.

After the ceremony, the family gathered outside. William's Galaxy friends, disguised in human form, handed him a card before quietly leaving. His family hugged him proudly.

Mr. Ross said, *"You're a genius, my friend. I have a surprise for you—here are the keys to your car. It has a new engine from Ford, fully checked. Consider it my gift."* *"Thank you very much,"* William replied.

Grandma Virginia added, *"Now it's my turn. You are the oldest of our grandsons. Here is a bank card. Whenever*

you need money, you may withdraw freely."
William kissed her forehead.

Mr. Carlos II then announced, *"My gift is a party at our club. Everyone, let's go. We have another limo for anyone who wants to ride separately."*

At the club, music filled the hall. Mr. Carlos's son stopped the orchestra and took the microphone:
"Attention, everyone! Tonight we celebrate Dr. William Roberts, the college's honor student. He is part of our family. Now, I present Dr. William Roberts!"

William stepped forward:
"Today is historic in my life. I am happy, but as a doctor, I also feel sadness when I cannot save lives. Yesterday's news of the London train tragedy reminded me that angels walk among us—sometimes strangers with qualities that reveal their true nature. Perhaps angels were there helping. Tonight, I thank my family, my grandparents, and all of you for giving me joy. Let us celebrate together."

Applause rang out. The orchestra resumed, and William danced with Mr. Ross's daughter. The party lasted until 2:30 in the morning. Dr. Carlos, tired after a few whiskies, slept in the limo on the way home.

The next day, the family woke late. Over breakfast, Dr. Carlos told William, *"The Alberton family loves you. You'll be one of the richest doctors. They're remodeling a downtown building, and your office will be there rent-free. A normal medical office costs about twenty-five hundred pounds a month, but yours will be provided."*

William replied, *"Dad, in my first year, I must work in the hospital. While I do that, I'd like you to run the office in my*

name until I finish my internship."
Carlos thought for a moment. *"Don't worry, son. You'll succeed. Rich patients come downtown, and those doctors charge a lot. You'll do the same."*
Lorena added, *"Carlos specializes in lungs, William in hearts—you'll both be in demand."*

Days later, Mr. Ross gifted William a fully restored car with a new engine, transmission, tires, paint, and leather seats. William admired it like new, thanking him deeply. At home, Lorena marveled at it too. William hugged her. *"Mom, you've been with me through hardships and joys. You're the best mother anyone could have."*

The family discussed enlarging the garage to fit two cars. William offered to pay for the renovation, and Carlos agreed to arrange it through hospital construction contacts.

On December 23rd, William visited his grandmother, Virginia, who was coughing up black fluid. He assured her the treatment was working, and she felt better. Her son Jack arrived and thanked William, calling him "a supernatural doctor." He also asked William to examine his wife after Christmas for gynecological problems. William agreed, writing medication for her in the meantime.

Jack then asked, *"How is your car running?"*
"Great—like a new car," William replied with a smile.

Chapter 11: Family Ties and Second Chances

William returned home, picked up the newspaper left at the front door, and began to read. To his surprise, a big headline caught his attention: **Camila had divorced after just ten months of marriage.**

As he skimmed further, he noticed a piece about himself—his recent achievement at college, where the dean presented him with an award. While William was absorbed in the paper, his mother was upstairs on the second floor, instructing the service girls about household tasks.

She called down to him, "Rossi, your aunt we were talking about yesterday, said that if you receive a package, it was sent by her. I asked whether she had sent it to the college or to the house. She said it was addressed to the college. That's not a problem—it will arrive after Christmas."

"Mom, did you read the newspapers?" William asked.

"Yes," she replied. "Your father and I spoke about it. That girl was always proactive in school, but she should have waited a little longer before marrying. She had no experience in life, and now she has to face the consequences. I do hope her future will be brighter and that she learns to be wiser next time."

"Where are Dad and Nolan?" William asked.

"They went shopping for the grandparents and the family," his mother explained. "Your father also spoke with the construction workers. They'll be here next Monday to start the garage work. Oh, and your grandma in the U.K.

called—she said she'll phone you tonight. She loved her Christmas present. Olivia also called; she couldn't make it to the ceremony, but she'll arrive tomorrow from France. She asked if she could spend Christmas with us. Of course, I told her she doesn't even need to ask. She's always welcome in our home."

William smiled. "I sent her a Christmas card, too. She wants us to visit Germany."

"Yes," his mother said. "I told her we'd likely plan that trip next year after your graduation. But remember, Nolan's graduation is also in May."

"That's fine, Mom. Aunt Olivia can use the spare room; it's big enough."

"They'll only be here for Christmas or maybe two days," his mother continued. "After that, they have other plans. I think she wants to see Rossi in Germany. You're right, my son—I'll have the big rooms prepared."

Just then, the doorbell rang. It was the deliveryman.

"Go open the garage and put the beer and whisky bottles in there," his mother instructed. "The rest, have the staff bring to the kitchen."

As William followed her orders, she added, "Let me ask you something. Mr. Carlos II probably doesn't have many grandchildren around him, does he?"

"Yes, Mother, he has two daughters, not sons."

"I see. That explains why he's so fond of you."

"Mom, his daughters love their grandfather, but they're very independent. That can sometimes be a problem. I must call him today. Mr. Lorena says he may want me for Christmas, but I hope not—he probably has other plans."

His mother nodded thoughtfully. "By the way, Aunt Emma said she will be here with Grandma for Christmas. This is going to be a wonderful holiday for everyone in the house."

William asked about his grandmother.

"She's fine," his mother said. "I spoke to her yesterday. She asked about you, and I told her you were busy with college. She understood."

Just then, the heat from the cookstove reminded her that she had left the percolator by the sink, filled with coffee and water, ready to be boiled.

"Mom, when the coffee is ready, I'll take a cup," William said.

"Of course, son," she replied.

A short while later, Dr. Carlos returned home with Nolan.

"Hi, sweetheart," his mother greeted him.

"Hello, my son," his father replied warmly.

She asked about the family, and he answered, "They're fine, thank you. I saw everyone except my brother—he's on vacation. Your parents will arrive on Christmas Eve with my sister and her two grown kids. Remind me tomorrow to buy some presents."

"I will," she said.

"Tomorrow is Saturday, right?" he asked.

"Yes, and Monday will be December twenty-third. I don't work that day, so I'll have time to shop."

Later that evening, William received an urgent call from Galaxies. There was an emergency. He excused himself, saying goodnight to his parents, and headed upstairs. On the second floor, Nolan was waiting.

"William, I have a problem with algebra," Nolan said.

"I'll work out three sample problems for you," William assured him. "That way, you'll understand how to solve the rest."

"Okay, thanks," Nolan replied.

William then called Mr. Carlos.

"Hello?" his grandfather answered.

"Grandpa, it's William."

"Hi, son. I'm glad you called. Are you doing well?"

"Yes, Grandpa. How are you?"

"I'm fine. Jack told me his wife isn't feeling well. Can you come by around a quarter past nine? John will pick you up."

"Alright, Grandpa. I'll take a shower and be ready."

Later, John, the driver, arrived, and William left for Jack's house. Inside, Jack's wife, Maya, was lying down in pain.

"She has severe stomach pain," Jack explained.

William examined her carefully and diagnosed ulcers. He prescribed medication and sent John to the pharmacy.

"Maya," he said gently, "you'll feel sharp pain now, but afterward it will improve." He administered an injection. She cried out, but soon after, the medicine began working. William explained the treatment: "Take two tablespoons every two hours. Tomorrow you may see some blood when you use the bathroom—don't panic, that's part of the process."

A nurse from Galaxies was assigned to stay overnight and continue her care.

Jack looked relieved. "Now I understand why Dad prefers not to take her to the hospital. We have the best doctor right here."

Grandpa added proudly, "My grandson will probably be a millionaire in three years. Every time I see his skill, I know patients will come to him daily. A doctor's visit already costs sixty pounds. He'll need another specialist to help him one day."

Jack then said, "William, since my parents will be away for Christmas as they usually are, how about my family spending Christmas Eve at your home?"

"Of course, I'd be glad," William replied.

Jack handed him a check. "This is your monthly payment—nine hundred pounds."

"Thank you," William said.

Jack's servant, Sera, brought coffee for them. They sat together until it was time for William to leave. Jack also gave him a gasoline card, saying his mother had insisted.

When William returned home, Aunt Emma and Grandma Evelyn had just arrived with Nova, the chauffeur. William embraced them warmly.

"I've heard so much about you," Aunt Emma said. "I wanted to attend your ceremony, but I wasn't feeling well. I think it was the flu."

"Well, you came at the right time, Aunt," William reassured her.

Grandma Evelyn added, "We're all doing well, thank God."

William then gave Aunt Emma a Christmas card with a check inside. She opened it in surprise.

"Five thousand pounds?!" she exclaimed.

"It's my turn to take care of you," William said with a smile.

He examined her, discovering she had bronchitis. He prescribed medicine and gave her an injection. "You need rest for at least four days, Aunt. Work from home—it's too cold outside."

"You're right," she admitted. "The injection made me a bit drowsy, too."

When Nova returned with the medicine, William explained the dosage and wished her a quick recovery.

Before leaving, Aunt Emma said, "I'll return after Christmas. In this box are presents for everyone. Lorena, check it soon—you'll find something special inside."

"Thank you, Aunt," Lorena replied warmly.

William smiled. "We'll see you soon. Let me know tomorrow how you're feeling."

And with that, the family's Christmas preparations continued, filled with love, concern, and anticipation for the days ahead.

Christmas Eve

The next day was Christmas Eve. Olivia had just received a call from downtown, where she was staying at a hotel, asking if someone could pick her up and bring her home.

Lorena turned to her son.
"William, we're going to the hotel to pick up your aunt."
"Okay, Mom," William replied. "I'll use your car. The trunk is bigger, and she's probably bringing a lot of things."

Ten minutes later, they left. William drove because he knew the downtown area better than his mother. They reached Kleber Square in Strasbourg and stopped at Olivia's hotel.

Lorena went inside to the front desk and asked for Olivia. The clerk called her, and after hanging up, he said, "She's on her way down."

Five minutes later, Olivia entered the reception hall. She hugged Lorena and then turned to William.
"This is my nephew?" she asked.
"Yes," Lorena smiled. "This is William."
Olivia hugged him warmly. "You look exactly like my brother."
"I told you so," Lorena said with a laugh.

They went outside, and a bellboy brought Olivia's suitcases, loading them into the trunk. She tipped him, and they drove back to Lorena's house.

On the way, Lorena and Olivia chatted. At home, William teased, "Aunt Olivia, you're taller than me. Everyone in the family is tall except Rossi. She's about Mom's height. Our father was six feet six."
"And you, William? How tall are you?" Olivia asked.
"Six feet four."

Just then, Nolan came in from skiing. Lorena introduced him.
"This is my son, Olivia."
"I'm glad to meet you," Olivia said.
"Mom, I'm hungry. Do you have something to eat?" Nolan asked.
"Yes, Lisa is in the kitchen," Lorena replied.

Olivia settled in and said, "I'll be here for three days, but I must leave for Germany afterward. My husband Peter is already there with the girls at Rossi's house."
"Rossi wants us to visit her, too," Lorena added. "But we

have plans for next year, after William graduates. His graduation is in December, so we'll have time."

They carried Olivia's suitcases upstairs, where Lorena had prepared a room.
"Olivia, you have beautiful hair," Lorena remarked.
"I dyed it black," Olivia explained. "The gray was coming in. How about you?"
"I dye mine too," Lorena admitted.

Olivia asked curiously, "How do German people treat the French in Germany? I spoke to Rossi, who's been living there for ten years, and she says she hasn't had any problems."
Lorena frowned. "I just want to be sure before traveling. When I first came here in 1944, there were still many issues with Germans in certain towns."
Olivia reassured her, "I don't think you'll have problems now. My brother-in-law is German, well-respected, and high-ranking in the military. They live in a good community, and times have changed. The younger generation is different."

The next morning was cold and crisp—Christmas Eve. Olivia woke with tears on her cheeks after dreaming that her husband had a car accident. Shaken, she rose quietly so as not to disturb Nolan, whose room was nearby. She considered calling Rossi before the household was fully awake.

As she was thinking, there was a knock at the door. She opened it to find Lorena.
"You're already up? It's almost eight o'clock. Come down for breakfast. I need the kids to help me bring in two more dining tables. Last night, I found an order in one of my aunt's boxes for twenty guest dinners!"

"I'll come as soon as I change," Olivia said.

Lorena went downstairs and called the restaurant.
"Mr. Joni, this is Mrs. Lorena. Do you still have my reservation for twenty guests for dinner?"
"Yes, ma'am. What time would you like it served?"
"Six-thirty."
"Perfect. We'll send staff with everything you need by four-thirty."

Lorena prepared the dining room, decorated beautifully with red tablecloths, Christmas ornaments, and angel formations on the ceiling. Evelyn soon came down.
"Good morning, Mom," Lorena greeted her.
"Good morning. I slept well," Evelyn replied.

Meanwhile, William and Nolan were outside painting the new garage door. William's car was parked inside. His grandmother stepped out, and he kissed her cheek.
"I love you, Grandma."
"You're the tallest of all my grandsons," she smiled.

By four-thirty, Emma Louise arrived.
"Lorena, do you need more seats?" she asked.
"Yes, about five more."
Emma quickly arranged for chairs to be brought from a warehouse nearby.

Soon after, Jack Alberton and his family arrived in a limo. William greeted them at the door. Inside, Lorena and her husband welcomed them warmly. Jack's wife, with red hair and sea-blue eyes, admired the decorations. Their twin daughters, both blonde, followed them in. Waiters served drinks while William and Jack went to the bar.

John, the chauffeur, delivered a case of whisky and fine wine.

"Thank you, Jack," William said.

"Put it in the kitchen, John," Jack instructed, "and then have a beer."

More guests arrived, including Dr. Carlos's colleagues and William's college friends. Musicians played soft, cheerful music as everyone mingled.

At six-forty-five, the guests gathered at the dining table, and dinner was served. Afterward, Olivia stood and announced, "Tonight, we are fortunate to have among us one of France's most famous singers—Mrs. Emma Louise."

Emma rose gracefully. "Thank you, ladies and gentlemen. It's my pleasure to be here with my family tonight."

William interrupted politely, "Aunt Emma, would you sing 'Silent Night' for us?"

"Well, I haven't sung in two years," she hesitated. "But tonight is special. William is like the son I never had, so I will."

She joined the musicians and sang beautifully. The guests applauded loudly.

The party was lively and warm, filled with doctors, family, and friends. Then came William's biggest surprise— Camila arrived with her mother.

William walked quickly to greet them.

"Welcome to my home. Please come in."

Her mother approached Lorena and her husband.

"Lorena, this is a gift for William from my husband and

me."
"Thank you, Mrs. Locksheed," Lorena said warmly.

Meanwhile, William escorted Camila to her mother, then returned to Jack and his friends. The evening carried on joyfully, with every guest enjoying the celebration.

Two days later, Olivia had to leave for the airport. In the morning, William asked her what time she would be flying to Frankfurt. She replied, "Two-thirty. I must be at the airport. Let me call a limo for you."

William asked, "Doesn't that cost too much money?"

Olivia smiled. "Not for you, my dear nephew. That is my adopted grandfather's business."

"Who is your grandfather?" William asked. Lorena, who was present, replied, "The third millenary of France."

Olivia was surprised. "What? Oh! I've heard about him. He owns a car parts factory in the U.K."

"My dear nephew, you are young, and you can achieve the best in your life," she told William.

"Thank you, Aunt Olivia," he replied. He called the limo, and ten minutes later returned. "It will be here at one-thirty this afternoon."

Olivia drew in a deep breath, relieved at the thought of soon seeing her family.

Two days later, William told his mother he had to do some research at the college for two days. He left in his car, as he had a new project on the galaxies. There was a major

doctors' convention on the subject, and he was also
scheduled to be awarded for his services at the Galaxy's
Hospital. He would return to college on February 10, 1965.
It was his final year—only six more months of classroom
studies remained, followed by a year of practical training.
Though he had already completed all the required theses
and was technically a doctor, the college rules required the
full term.

Lorena's older sister was two years her senior, and her
younger brother lived in the U.K., though neither often
contacted family—not even their mother, Mrs. Evelyn.
Evelyn told Lorena she wanted to see them. Before the war,
she had last seen both Julia and Adrien—Julia had been a
teacher and school rector, while Adrien worked in the
military. Lorena asked, "But do you even know where they
live?"

Her mother replied, "I know one person who might. My
older grandson, Peter, is Julia's son. He once wrote a letter
when he was in a German camp. I must look for those
letters. As soon as I find them, I'll call you."

Meanwhile, William traveled to the galaxies. He had made
many trips there and even had his own vehicle. They
traveled by air to attend the celebration and convention
near Loopy, the central governors' hub of the galaxies. All
spoke the same language and shared a culture. The journey
took only two hours.

William traveled with four galaxy doctors and was to be
awarded as one of the best surgeons. Two nurses also
accompanied them, including Tatty, who also worked with
William on Earth. Though young by galaxy standards
(forty years old), she had the appearance of a beautiful
woman with blonde hair, sea-blue eyes, and a slender build,

standing five feet six inches tall. William admired her greatly.

After the convention, Tatty took him near where she had been raised. William noticed that their schools, though small by Earth's standards, were built into mountainsides. Only the fronts were visible, while the rest extended deep inside the rock. Most galaxy cities were subterranean, built this way for protection from extreme weather—temperatures that could plummet below freezing or soar to hundreds of degrees, along with toxic winds and gas hurricanes.

They were far more advanced than Earth, particularly in medicine. Earth did not even have half its technology.

William later returned to his college, completed his project, and then went home. Three days later, his mother told him, "Your Grandma Elizabeth is very sick in Manchester Hospital. I spoke to your Uncle Leo Roberts. He says that despite her faith in God, her spirit is weakening. Her heart condition worries her, and she fears she will pass away like your grandfather did."

William called her, promising to visit in two days. In truth, he planned to go sooner. That very night, he went to the hospital with the galaxy nurse. Knowing Elizabeth's veins were clogged with calcium, he carefully administered an intravenous medicinal fluid to help dissolve the deposits. Within two days, her blood circulation began improving.

The next morning, she awoke feeling better and asked the nurse for tea. Surprised by her recovery, the nurse informed the doctor. He checked Elizabeth's condition and was astonished. "Her blood pressure was very high yesterday. Now it's nearly normal. What medicine was she given?"

The nurse showed him the chart. "It was prescribed last night."

The doctor said, "We'll continue this treatment. It seems to be cleansing her system. Though I've never seen this medicine before, it is working. If her blood pressure remains stable, she can go home tomorrow."

The next day, William called his grandmother. "How are you feeling?"

She replied, "Much better. The doctor says if my pressure stays normal, I can go home tomorrow."

"That's wonderful, Grandma. I'll see you on Saturday."

Meanwhile, Dr. Carlos had a hospital convention in Singapore on February 20, accompanied by his wife, Mrs. Phillips, to learn about new surgical technologies. Nolan stayed with his grandparents while William traveled to Manchester to see his grandmother.

He got off the train in Rochdale, where Uncle Leo was waiting. "How are you, William?"

"I'm fine, thank you, Uncle," he replied. They drove to the hospital, where William greeted his grandmother warmly. Dr. John, her attending doctor, congratulated William on his future career. After checking her, Dr. John declared that she could go home if she wished.

The next evening, Elizabeth returned home. William handed her the prescribed pills. "Take two a day for two weeks, and check your blood pressure daily. You'll get stronger."

"For the first time in months, I feel like a heavy weight has been lifted from my chest," she said with relief.

That night, William and the galaxy nurse once again administered advanced treatment while Elizabeth slept. By the next morning, she felt so well that she insisted on making breakfast with Mia, the maid. She told her son Joe about a dream she'd had: William, dressed as a doctor, with a nurse beside him, administering medicine to her.

Joe chuckled, "That's a nice dream, Mom. But William isn't practicing yet."

William only smiled.

Later, his cousins Abigail and Joe Junior visited. Abigail congratulated him on his success. "I saw your name in the newspaper!"

"Thank you," William replied kindly.

The next afternoon, William prepared to leave. Abigail's boyfriend dropped by, and the family gathered in the kitchen. At around two o'clock, William told Uncle Joe, "I need to catch the three o'clock train. I have much to do."

Joe agreed and drove him to the station. Elizabeth walked them to the door. William hugged her. "I'll call you tomorrow, Grandma. Goodbye."

Chapter 12: The Making of a Doctor

William returned home after two and a half hours of traveling by train. When he arrived at London station, his mother was waiting for him, relieved to see him. Earlier that morning, she had received a call from her aunt Emma, telling her that William's grandmother was in the hospital, and she had been worried since.

William hugged his mother, giving her that reassuring smile of his that always made her feel better. On the way home, she mentioned his grandmother's health problems. "Mom," he said gently, "she'll be fine."

The weather that night was cool. William went upstairs, saying, "I'm going to take a shower. Dinner's in the refrigerator, right?"
"Okay, Mom."

On his way up, he saw Nolan in his room, with their father helping him with some homework. Both came out when they noticed William. His father asked, "How is your grandmother doing?"
"She's out of the hospital," William replied. Nolan hugged him tightly.
"I missed you! One of your friends, Louis, came by looking for you. He told Mom some things and left you a letter."
William rubbed Nolan's head with a smile. "Thanks. Let me take my shower first."

Later, William came downstairs. His mother was in the kitchen. "I just made some fresh coffee," she said.
"Thank you, Mom."
"Your friend was here two days ago. He left some college letters for you—they're in your office."
"Okay, Mom. I'm starving, though. The only thing I had

was a tuna fish sandwich and coffee on the train three hours ago."

William sat at the table while his mother served him dinner. "There's nothing like a home-cooked meal," he said. But he also knew his mother would feel better if they visited his grandmother that night. After eating, he said, "Mom, let's go see Grandma."
"I'll get ready too," she replied.

Five minutes later, they left for the hospital.

At the hospital, visiting hours were already over, but William had his doctor's license, so they were allowed inside. They went to the second floor. Mrs. Lorena was clearly worried about her mother, and William could sense her emotions.

Inside the room, the hospital doctor had just finished examining his grandmother. "We tested her lungs. There's inflammation in her throat. I've prescribed antibiotics," the doctor explained before leaving.

William asked his mother to wait outside. He then checked his grandmother himself with his special stethoscope. He quickly realized she had pneumonia. This wasn't something ordinary doctors could detect with regular instruments—it required the advanced device William had brought from the Galaxies. Only two of these instruments existed, and he always kept his in his pocket.

He carefully put his grandmother into a deep sleep and administered a special medication from the Galaxies. When the nurse returned with the prescribed pills, William told her, "Give them to me, I'll take care of it." After she left, he slipped the pills into his pocket—his grandmother didn't need them anymore.

When he finished, he found his mother in the cafeteria. "She's sleeping now. Tomorrow she should be better. Let's go home."

That night, William left for the Galaxies. He had received a call for urgent hospital work. To avoid suspicion on Earth, he left a clone in his bed. This nurse-clone was connected to him mentally and could answer anyone in his voice if needed.

The Galaxy's city lay underground, filled with massive hospitals, advanced technology, and even secret military facilities. At one of the military hospitals near the largest airfield, William had three surgeries scheduled. For two days, he worked nonstop with nurses and doctors, performing highly advanced operations with equipment far beyond Earth's technology—computers, cameras, and detailed automated records.

Meanwhile, on Earth, his mother had no idea he was gone. His clone had left a note saying he had gone to medical school. When William finally returned, his mother was surprised to see him. "I didn't hear you this morning when I made coffee," she said.

"I'm sorry, Mom," William answered. "I had to be up very early to join the other doctors."
She sighed but smiled. "It's alright, son. Just don't disappear without telling me again. I only worry."
"Of course, Mom," he said.

Upstairs, Nolan was laughing in the bathroom, bathing his dog. William peeked in, amused. Nolan looked up,

grinning. "Guess what? My uncle Jace from New York is coming! Dad's going to pick him up at the airport, and he'll be staying at Grandma's house with his wife and kids."
"That's great news," William replied.

Later, William opened his college mail and found a letter with a check for five thousand pounds—payment for his new filing system invention. The letter explained that he would receive ten thousand pounds yearly for the next four years.

Meanwhile, Nolan was preparing for his high school graduation, scheduled for May 20, 1965. He also had a prom coming up. His friend Lydia visited, returning a book and homework she had borrowed. Nervously, she asked Nolan if he would be her escort for prom. Nolan happily agreed.

That afternoon, William and his father took Nolan to the park for soccer practice. Afterward, William went to a stadium with his father and brother to watch a championship match between France and the UK.

There, William noticed an old high school friend, Adrian Kennedy, struggling to breathe due to asthma. His face had turned red, and he was in distress. William quickly checked him, administered treatment, and rushed him to the hospital with the help of friends. The ER doctor later confirmed Adrian would be fine, thanks to William's quick action.

Adrian's mother thanked William with tears in her eyes.
"Who are you?" she asked.
"I'm just a medical student," William replied humbly.
"But you saved my son," she said gratefully.

Though modest, William knew his time on Earth and in the Galaxies was shaping him into one of the finest doctors of his time.

Some of the galaxies had not yet been explored, while others had been abandoned. In some cases, great disasters had wiped out entire populations. William took his girlfriend, Tratty, on a flight to one of these galaxies. Some of them were extremely dangerous, as criminals from other galaxies often built bases there to commit mob-related crimes, much like on Earth.

As they flew in their cars, they noticed an old base. They landed cautiously, narrowing their eyes to see if anyone was around. To stay hidden, they hired a small spaceship in an area invisible to the eye, covering it with a parachute. They soon realized the base was near a cave. William said, "Come back in. I'm going to bring the spaceship." He drove for a short while until the path narrowed, forcing them to stop.

They had to wear heavy military-style suits designed for extreme cold, with boots and gloves. The galaxy's temperature was fifteen degrees below zero, but the suits were heated. On their backs, they carried equipment with two small rocket boosters, allowing them to fly short distances if needed. They were also armed with weapons.

Continuing into the cave, they descended about one hundred feet and reached what appeared to be old homes. William examined the area carefully, and then they decided to walk further. After half an hour, they discovered a large building. "This may have been an old school," Tratty suggested. She pulled out an emergency light, as it was getting dark.

Inside the building, they were surprised to find an old religious priest. Remarkably, he spoke the same language as Tratty's family. The priest invited them to join him, taking them down into the building by a special elevator. They emerged in a vast plaza, where many people were gathered. Near a train station, the priest's spaceship awaited, and soon they flew to the city. After a twenty-minute flight, they landed.

The priest introduced himself as **Rohullah**, and to William's surprise, he spoke three languages fluently. He translated for William so that he could communicate. After a pleasant lunch at the priest's home, they boarded an underground train, which sped along at 350 miles per hour toward the Great City. It was said to be the most modern city in all the galaxies. The journey took half an hour.

On the train, Tratty turned to William. "I think we should go look for a certain place—it could be very interesting to you."
William studied her face. "Do you know this place?"
She nodded. "Yes. My parents once lived here. We even have some relatives in a city called Notsob. I have the GPS."

The priest, seated a few rows ahead, overheard and agreed to accompany them. When the train finally arrived, William and Tratty stepped onto the platform, awestruck by the city's dazzling lights. The moving platform carried crowds effortlessly toward various exits while announcements played over the speakers.

As they left the station, William received a mental message from his clone back on Earth. His final exams at medical school were approaching in just two weeks—he would soon need to return.

Meanwhile, the priest led them onto a moving bridge that connected to different streets. They then boarded a flying car, paying with a coded plastic card linked to the city's computer system. Tratty reviewed her notes in a pocket-sized notebook as they flew for ten minutes. Eventually, they arrived at a grand house.

The priest touched the door, which opened automatically. Inside, Tratty whispered to William, "Look up—you're about to meet someone important. She's part of your life."

Puzzled, William asked, "How could she be part of my life?"
"Just wait," Tratty replied.

A lady in a blue-and-white dress appeared. She introduced herself as **Princess Arellano of the Three Stars Galaxy**. "Welcome, everyone. Please join us for dinner in the Blue Salon."

That evening, they dined on an elaborate eight-course meal with the Princess, the priest, and even a governor from another galaxy. After dinner, the Princess spoke privately with the priest on the balcony.

Finally, she revealed the truth. Taking a deep breath, she said, "I donated William's embryo. My husband preserved it. After the war forced us to flee our galaxy twenty years ago, we came here, and eventually to Earth. During one trip to the U.K., I saw a woman with her husband. She wore a wedding ring. One night, we implanted the embryo. That woman became William's mother."

The priest was stunned. "Do you realize what this means? His mother has no idea. She believes her husband is William's father, yet he was infertile."

"Yes," the Princess said softly. "I've watched William grow up. His mother will never know the truth. But he deserves to."

They debated how William might react. Would he feel betrayed, or would he accept his true origins? The Princess thought Tratty might be the best person to help him understand.

The next day, William and Tratty explored a massive cave filled with ferocious creatures—flying black bears with incredible strength. William experienced his first real combat, using laser weapons to defend himself.

Soon after, William returned home to Earth. His mother, Mrs. Lorena, greeted him with concern. "Something happened last week. I called you, but your machine cut off."

"I'm sorry, Mom," William explained. "I was in the operating room for an emergency."

She handed him several letters. Nolan came running to hug him, excited about his upcoming graduation.

Later, William attended a meeting with Mr. Carlos II and other doctors. They proudly presented him with his own medical office in a newly renovated building downtown, worth millions. His grandmother had gifted him all the equipment. Though only twenty-one, William was already recognized as one of the brightest and most promising doctors.

That evening, the family celebrated at the luxurious **Carlos Castle Restaurant**, where Mr. Carlos II introduced William to the city's elite. William's stepfather, Dr. Carlos Phillis, spoke emotionally about his talents, intelligence, and humility.

Finally, William addressed the gathering:
"Tonight marks the end of medical school and the beginning of my journey as a doctor. I thank my grandparents, who believed in me long before I believed in myself. I promise to dedicate my life to healing others."

The hall erupted in applause. Mrs. Lorena wept tears of joy, proud of her son who had achieved so much so young.

Preparations for his graduation ceremony began immediately, with family from across the country arriving to celebrate. William's journey was only beginning, but he had already become a doctor, a healer, and someone destined for much greater truths than he yet realized.

The next day, William woke up early. His grandmother, Elizabeth Roberts, was already at Lorena's house in Dijon. Lorena's mother, Mrs. Evelyn, and her aunt, Emma Louise, were also there, all prepared for the Graduation Ceremony. It was to take place at the **University of Edinburgh Medical School**.

William, too, had to prepare himself, though his mind was on other matters as well. Kwon was leaving for vacation, sponsored by the company that supplied office accessories. It was the same company that had adopted Kwon's idea for the new file system at the College. His first stop would be

Germany, where he planned to visit his aunt Rossi. From there, he would travel to Spain to tour hospitals and observe how they operated. Kwon also intended to dedicate time to his work in the Galaxies, especially the cloning projects he was developing for William. He would also be honored at the great **Galaxy Doctor Convention**, attended by the most prominent hospital leaders—though no one truly knew Kwon. These same leaders would later visit the College as friends, along with William's Galaxy nurses, who worked with him. They, too, were planning grand ceremonies across the Galaxies as soon as William's teams arrived.

Meanwhile, Doctor Carlos and Lorena had arranged a large breakfast at a nearby restaurant. Once the food was ready and the family gathered around the table, William's grandmother, Elizabeth, smiled warmly and said, "I am so happy to be here to see my grandson graduate as a doctor. I only wish my husband could be here, too. But wherever he is now, I'm sure he is proud and happy to know our grandson has become a doctor."

As everyone began breakfast, Mrs. Lorena added, "Well, I thank God for this day. Thank you, everyone, for coming to celebrate my son's graduation as a doctor. This is a great blessing, and I truly appreciate William's father's family for making the sacrifice to be here today. Thank the Lord."

Chapter 13: Celebration and Surprises

Someone looked through the small glass window at the front door, and to Kwok's surprise, it was **Camila Locksheed**. The service girl quickly opened the door and said, "Mrs. Lorena, Mrs. Camila is here." She then escorted Camila into the living room and told her, "Please wait here, Mrs. Lorena will be with you shortly."

Camila sat down politely. The service girl asked, "Would you like something to drink? Coffee or tea?"
"Yes, I'll take a cup of coffee," Camila replied. "I'll be right back," the girl said.

Soon, Mrs. Lorena entered the room. Camila stood up to greet her.
"Hi, Mrs. Lorena, how are you?"
"I'm fine, thank you," Lorena replied. "What brings you here today?"
"I saw yesterday's newspaper with William's graduation picture. He was named the number one medical school doctor. I came to bring him this card and also ask if I could attend the graduation ceremony tonight at the College. If there are no extra passes, don't worry—my uncle, Professor July, teaches at the College, so I could get one from him. I just wanted to know if William would be alright with me being there. I don't think he would mind."

Lorena nodded. "Let me call William." She called upstairs, "William, can you come here please?"
"Okay, I'll be there, Mom," he answered.

A moment later, William came down.
"Hi Camila, how are you?"
"Fine, thank you. How about your son?"
"He's doing well."

"And how is your mother?" William asked kindly.
"She's fine now. After my father died, she was very sick
for a while, but she has recovered."

Camila handed him a card. "This is for you. I'd like to
attend your graduation ceremony tonight at the College, if
you don't mind."
William smiled. "No problem. I'll be very busy tonight
with friends coming from all over, so I may not have much
time to spend with anyone, but you're welcome to come."
"That's okay," Camila replied. "My uncle will be there
too."
"Yes, I know your uncle, Professor July Ron. He works in
the laboratories."
"Well, I must go now. I'll see you later. Goodbye, and
thank you," Camila said as she left.

Meanwhile, **Nolan** was preparing to enter college for the
fall semester. He and William began discussing Nolan's
space studies. William explained, "Here on Earth, people
don't really understand the true life of the Galaxies. The
military—USF—has created stories that aren't true. They
claim the people are green with big eyes, but in reality, just
like Earth has people of different races—black, yellow,
white—other planets have their own variations. God
created not only this world but the Universe too. Believe it
or not, beings from the Galaxies come here every day, but
they make themselves invisible. Their spaceships are
extremely fast. They often take natural resources like wood,
fruit, and even ocean water. They purify the water and use
it to make medicine. Their technology is far more advanced
than ours."

William continued, "Some Galaxies have poor vegetation
and low oxygen, so their plants grow differently. They also
disable electronic equipment when they enter Earth's orbit,

avoiding radars or defense systems. They come here when they need something. I once saw a movie about the Air Force in Alaska, where the commander ordered an investigation into a possible UFO crash. The soldiers discovered a disc-shaped spaceship and brought it back to base. Inside, they found a creature—they couldn't tell if it was a man or a woman. They locked it away, thinking it was a monster. Later in the film, the creature grew into a giant and attacked the soldiers. On Earth, no one really knows what's true, but these stories spread."

Nolan asked, "So do you believe normal life exists in the Galaxies?"
William replied, "Yes. I've read many books about them. They have civilizations just like we do, with genetics and hospitals, some even more advanced than ours. But here on Earth, people prefer to imagine them as green monsters who know nothing."

It was a pleasant day. The windows were open, and a breeze played with the ends of Nolan's long black hair. Just then, Mrs. Lorena came upstairs and knocked on the door. "Come in, Mom," William said.
She entered and told him, "The limo is outside."
"Yes, Mom," William replied. "They came early because there's a lot of work today. Several colleges have graduation ceremonies at the same time. Let me get ready. I'll see you later, Nolan."
"Okay, my brother," Nolan said.

Downstairs, the house was filled with family members bringing gifts. William's grandmother was ready, along with his uncles. Soon, two more limos arrived. William got into one to head to the College early for a private ceremony—the **Doctors' Socratic Oath**—before the public graduation began.

By 5 o'clock, Mrs. Emma Louise, Evelyn (Lorena's mother), Dr. Carlos, Lorena, and Nolan were all dressed and ready. They entered one limo, while Elizabeth (William's grandmother), her two sons, and the rest of the family—including Emma Louise, Evelyn, Olivia, and Rossi—took another. The driver asked, "Is everyone here?" "Yes," Emma Louise replied. "You may go now."

Neighbors stood outside watching as the limos departed for the College. At the same time, Camila, her mother, and two of William's high school friends also made their way to the ceremony.

The College parking lot was crowded, with police directing traffic. Inside the Spectrum, the seating was arranged carefully: the front rows for government officials and special guests, the second for College supporters, the third for religious figures, and the rest for families and friends. Among them were Mr. Carlos II and his wife, Jack's wife and daughters, the Mayor of Army Cameron, Plaids Hudson (a close friend of Mr. Carlos II), William's family, Camila and her mother, and William's old schoolmates, Jeremiah Maverick and Joseph Smith. Everyone was eager for the ceremony to begin.

The weather was slightly chilly. At 7 o'clock sharp, **Dean Mr. Adan R. Cooper** stepped forward and began:

"Ladies and gentlemen, and distinguished guests, it is with great pleasure that my staff, professors, and I present to you our new doctors. We wish them the best as they dedicate themselves to saving human lives. Some will remain here, while others will travel to different parts of the world. Each of them represents our College with pride.

Over the years, we have seen many types of students. Some are shy at first but grow into their confidence. Others are quick to engage and participate. Some come from families of doctors, carrying on the tradition. But this year, we have one very special student. He has proven himself exceptional. He completed his medical degree in just five years, and during his time here, he performed his first arm operation—a remarkable achievement for a student.

In his first year, he also worked in the Dean's office and developed a brilliant idea to improve our file system, which is now patented and used widely. He has performed numerous significant surgeries, some of which even senior doctors had never attempted. His name and picture are now part of this College's history.

I believe many of you tonight have already been his patients and can attest to his skill. It is now my honor to present to you the number one student of this College, our newest doctor, **Mr. William Roberts.**"

The audience rose to their feet, applauding with pride and admiration.

After all the guests were seated, William stepped forward and began his speech.

"First, I want to thank everyone who is here tonight. Above all, I thank the Lord God, who gave me this privilege to stand before you as a doctor. I also thank my parents, who made it possible for me to reach my goals.

To my Aunt, Mrs. Emma Louisa Schiffer—who has been like a second mother to me—you have believed in me since my days at Saint Michael Catholic School. I still remember the first time you told me, 'It's time to get a summer job. If you like the idea, I have one for you.' That was the best news I could have had as a teenager, because back then, every pound counted.

To my two grandmothers, Elizabeth and Evelyn, whom I love so dearly—this is a little secret I'll share with you all tonight: don't tell anyone, but they spoiled me a lot."
The audience laughed warmly.

"And of course, my mother—she carried me for nine months, worked hard all her life, and still came home to take care of me, helping me with my homework. For that alone, there is no money or gold in this world that could repay you. Thank you, Mom.

I also thank God for giving me a second family, who believe in me not just as a doctor but as a person. They offered me their love and adopted me as their grandson. It is my pleasure to introduce you to Mr. and Mrs. Carlos II, Virginia Alberton, and Mr. Jack Alberton, who is like another brother to me.

Finally, I would like to thank our College Dean, Mr. Dan Cooper, as well as all my professors and the staff. Thank you very much, and God bless you all."

The ceremony ended at eleven o'clock. Outside, in the Spectrum patio, William met with his family and friends. He asked the limousine drivers if they had the address for the hotel party.
"Yes, we do," they replied.

He then told his parents, "Please ride with Mr. and Mrs. Alberton's family—they have all the things prepared for the celebration." He also instructed the other guests to follow the first limo, which carried Mrs. Emma Louisa. In total, nine or ten limos traveled together.

Inside William's limo, Mr. Carlos II opened a champagne bottle and raised a toast. "This drink is for William and for all our families. I met him four years ago, and I quickly saw that his actions were like gold. He was never interested in money, but always in helping others. He is humble, kind, and ready to serve anyone in need. That is why my wife and I love him so much. Mrs. Lorena and Mr. Carlos Phillis, thank you for sharing your son with us."

William's stepfather responded warmly: "Thank you, Mr. Carlos II. It is a great joy to hear such heartfelt words. I came into William's life when he was about twelve years old, after his mother and I married. He accepted me and his stepbrother with love and no difference between us. Being a doctor myself, I knew he would one day become a great doctor—not only here, but across the country. I am proud to be part of his life. Let us share this drink. Thank you."

Just then, Robert, the driver, interrupted politely: "We've arrived." He parked the limo in front of the hotel entrance.

At the hotel, attendants guided everyone to the banquet hall. It was a large room, beautifully prepared for the celebration. The tables were labeled with names, and each guest found their place while waiters served drinks. About an hour later, the speaker announced:

"Ladies and gentlemen, the Governor of this city and other authorities are here tonight. It is my great pleasure to present to you Mrs. Emma Louisa Schiffer. She is well known as a leading businesswoman and the owner of this hotel. She will now open tonight's graduation celebration for William. Please welcome Mrs. Emma."

The crowd rose to its feet in applause.

Mrs. Emma smiled and said, "Please be seated. Well, ladies and gentlemen, tonight we celebrate…"

My nephew's graduation as a doctor is a great joy for the entire family. I know he will have a safe and successful life as a doctor. I am sure some of you here remember the cruelty of the Second World War. Many soldiers died because there were no doctors around. Let me tell you, I first met my nephew when he was ten years old. Because of the terrible war, families were separated in France and elsewhere. Even now, some families still do not know if their loved ones survived.

I used to travel a few times each year to Saint Michael Catholic School. On one of those visits, the Rector of the school told me, "Mrs. Emma, I have some important news for you. Your nephew is a very smart boy." I was so happy to hear that. He explained that William would have to move up from eighth grade to ninth grade. That day, I realized that our emotions can sometimes become our greatest resources in life, for they reveal so much about our true selves.

Later that summer, William started working in one of our stores. After about a week, the manager called me at home and said, "Mrs. Emma, the new boy you sent me is doing something different. I showed him the job, but he asked if he could reorganize all the plastic records differently—by number and series." The manager noticed it was much faster and easier to find any record that way. Since then, all our warehouses have adopted the same system. William was only fifteen years old at the time.

Then he went on to college. His mother was so happy when he earned two years of scholarships. But after that, she became worried because medical school is very expensive. I told her not to worry too much. During his second year of medical school, William broke the highest academic record ever set—one that had stood for twenty years. For that, the Governor awarded him a scholarship covering all his medical school expenses, and the College also gave him ten thousand pounds. Thanks to his brilliance, his education was fully funded. In just five years, he became a doctor.

But ladies and gentlemen, his best quality is not just his intelligence—it is his humility. He is always ready to serve anyone in need. I know he will become a very popular young doctor, one who truly cares for his patients. I am deeply proud. And now, I present to you my nephew, Doctor William Roberts.

Everyone rose from their seats and applauded. Some of his former roommates were also there.

"Good evening, ladies and gentlemen," William began. "You know how I felt listening to my Aunt Emma. She was the person I looked up to as a child, the one who gave me the push I needed to face the real world. At that time, I was my mother's only child, and my father had already passed away. My mother tried to return to her country, working hard to support us. She left the place where my father had brought her, and at the end of the war, our nation was struggling to recover. She was lucky to meet my Uncle Jaxon, who helped her get a little house. Two weeks later, she found work as a hospital nurse in Dijon.

Many of you know that the hospital was one of the only buildings left standing after the German bombings. My mother worked under very hard conditions, often with very limited supplies. After five years, she transferred to a new hospital that had just opened its doors.

What I want to say tonight is that life is never easy. I consider myself fortunate. Success does not come without hard work. Climbing to the top of the mountain takes effort, but it is possible. I hope the young students here tonight can take something from my story. Thank you to everyone here tonight."

Then he introduced the Governor of Strasbourg.

"Ladies and gentlemen," said Governor Bryson Cooper, "it is a pleasure to be here at this graduation. I listened to Doctor William's speech, and I must say he is brilliant. His words reminded me of my own youth, when I had many different ideas about life.

My father owned a transportation business at the French ports. He worked very hard, driving trucks. I had two brothers as well. My father gave the job to my uncle Leonardo, his older brother, but unfortunately, he drank too much. One day, instead of going to the waterside to pick up cargo, my uncle stopped at a bar and drank heavily. By chance, my father drove by and saw the truck parked outside. He went inside, found my uncle drunk, and immediately took the keys.

He then called another driver to bring the cargo truck to the same location. I was with my father that summer, working as his helper. He asked me to drive the truck back to the garage. I was only seventeen and had just a junior license. The truck had a manual transmission, but I had practiced in the yard before. When my mother saw me trying to park the truck, she ran out, shocked, and shouted, 'What are you doing driving this big truck?' I told her Dad had instructed me to do so.

My father always believed in hard work. He wanted me to take over his business one day, but I wanted to be a lawyer. I told him so, and while he was disappointed, he respected my decision. Eventually, my brother became an airplane mechanic, and my father accepted that his sons would choose different paths.

What I want to show you tonight is that William is an excellent example for young people. He worked hard, used his talent wisely, and paid his way through medical school with the recognition he earned. Even his professors were amazed at his achievements.

But tonight, there is also a surprise. William does not know this, but during his hospital training, he performed two operations that had never been done before in that hospital. Both patients were at high risk of dying, and even the senior doctors did not want to take the chance. But William stepped forward and saved both lives.

Those two patients are here tonight. Ladies and gentlemen, please welcome Mr. Eli Hudson and Mrs. Stella Presley."

The hall erupted in applause as the two came forward. Governor Cooper continued, "Doctor William, do you remember these two patients?"

"Yes, I do," William replied. "I remember discussing the risks with their families. Both had serious heart problems. The surgery lasted almost seven hours. My only goal was to save their lives."

Governor Cooper smiled. "And you did. Not only that, you also invented two medical instruments that are now produced in the United States and used in hospitals everywhere. On behalf of these two grateful patients, I am honored to present you with this gift—a brand new Mercedes-Benz."

The patients handed William the keys. Both said, "We thank you. We are here today because of you."

The celebration lasted until three o'clock in the morning. William then moved into his newly reconstructed apartment building. The second-floor flat was fully furnished, with a garage in the back for his new car. His old car remained at his mother's house. His medical office was scheduled to open in January 1966.

After his vacation in Germany, where he would visit his Aunt Rossi, and then Spain to study their hospital systems, William was ready to begin the next chapter of his life.

The next morning, he called the limo center and ordered two limousines—one for his grandmother traveling by train and another for visitors heading to the airport. Later that evening at dinner, his stepfather said, "Your mother, your brother, and I have a gift for you. It will be perfect for your new apartment. We've arranged for decorators to furnish it while you are away on vacation, so everything will be ready when you return."

William handed his mother the keys. "Thank you, Mom, Dad, and Nolan. I love you all."

His mother then asked, "When do you plan to leave for Germany?"

"This Thursday," William replied. "The plane leaves at nine o'clock. After that, I'll be in Spain."

They agreed to take care of the apartment preparations and help set up his medical office downtown while he was away. William hugged them all and said, "Thank you. I love you all."

Chapter 14: The Doctor Beyond Borders

William arrived at Frankfurt Airport in Germany, where his Aunt Rossi and her husband, Gerld, were waiting to receive him.

"Hi, Aunt Rossi," William greeted warmly.
She smiled and said, "This is my husband, Gerld."
"Glad to meet you, sir," William replied politely.

On the way home, Aunt Rossi asked, "How is your mother doing?"
"She's fine," William answered. "I think she mentioned that next summer she and my stepfather might stop here for a few days. They'll be vacationing in Italy, while my stepbrother will be in college around that time. How about you and your family, Aunt?"
"I'm doing well, working hard, with many patients to look after. I hear you already have an office?"
"Yes, I do. I also have a large apartment in the same building," William explained.
"I hope everything works out well for you," Rossi said.
"Congratulations, William," Gerld added.
"Thank you, sir," William replied.
"How was your trip?" Gerld asked.
"Fine, sir, it was only about an hour and a half."
"Well, here we are already," Gerld said as they arrived.

William stepped out of the car and looked around in admiration. "Aunt Rossi, this is a big mansion!"

They walked inside, and Aunt Rossi said, "We have plenty of space in this home." They sat in the living room, and fifteen minutes later, the service maid, Lillian, entered.
"Mrs. Rossi, the room is ready," she announced.

"Thank you, Lillian," Rossi said. "William, come with me, I'll show you your room."

William followed her upstairs with his suitcase. "This is your room. Get some rest, lunch will be served soon."
"Thank you, Aunt," he replied.

He unpacked and hung up his clothes. A little while later, Lillian knocked on his door.
"Mr. William, lunch is ready."
"Thank you, Lillian, I'll be down shortly."

At lunch, his two cousins joined him. Isaac, who had just returned from college, asked his mother, "Has my cousin arrived?"
"Yes," she replied. "He's on the second floor and will be down soon."

Theresa, his other cousin, had been playing tennis in the yard. She came in and greeted him.
"Hi, Cousin William, how are you?"
"I'm fine, thank you. How are your college studies going?"
"They're fine, though not too easy. I'd like to major in electrical engineering. At my college in Germany, we also have French newspapers in the library. I even saw your picture in one with a big headline calling you *The Genius Doctor*!"

William smiled. "You can do the same, Theresa. The important thing is to stay focused on your studies all the time. Forget about parties and movies while you're in college. Think of it this way: the struggle isn't forever. Once you finish, you'll have all the time in the world to enjoy other things. Most functions of our mind—feelings, reasoning, perception, judgment, and even self-awareness—are tied to memory. Memory is more permanent than matter itself. Our cells remember, and that's why habits, good or bad, can be so hard to change. Our memory is like money in the bank—you know it's there, and it guides your choices. If we learn to control our actions, we can master our lives and achieve better results."

Theresa looked at him in admiration. "William, I can see why they call you a genius."

The table fell silent as everyone listened to his words.

After lunch, Isaac and Theresa invited William to go sightseeing. "Would you like to come with us?" they asked.
"That sounds nice, thank you," William said. "Aunt, would you like to join us?"
"No," she replied with a smile. "Your uncle and I have things to take care of at home. You three go and have fun."

"We'll take my car," Theresa said proudly. "It's a convertible. My dad gave it to me for my high school graduation."
"That's a beautiful car," William said.
Isaac appeared from behind. "Alright, let's go. Our first stop is Heidelberg Castle."

They drove for about thirty minutes before arriving at the castle.
"I've heard about this place," William said, impressed. "It's something worth seeing."

They explored the castle, walked around, and stopped at a few shops for ice cream. William took many pictures. They returned home around eight in the evening. The weather was pleasant, about ten degrees warmer than usual for that time of year. William enjoyed the trip and felt happy to spend time with his father's side of the family.

The next day, his aunt drove him back to Frankfurt Airport. "Thank you, Aunt Rossi. I'll never forget the time I spent at your house," William said with tears in his eyes. They hugged tightly before he left. She stood watching him walk to the gate, her eyes filled with emotion. Seeing William reminded her of her brother, and she felt both proud and sad as he disappeared from view.

Two hours later, William boarded his flight to Barcelona, Spain. The journey took six hours, and upon landing at El Prat Airport, he went through immigration, collected his luggage, and searched for the exit. With the crowd of passengers, he stopped to ask someone where the tour guide's office was. They pointed him in the right direction, and William entered the office.

The person in charge, Francisco, greeted him. "Can I help you?"
William was surprised by his fluent English. "Yes, I have a reservation at Cotton House Hotel. I need to call them."
"Of course. You can use those phones over there."
"Thank you," William said, making the call.

"Hello, this is Cotton House Hotel, how may I help you?"
"Yes, this is Dr. William Roberts. I have a reservation."
"One moment, sir, let me check… Yes, I found your booking. Are you at the airport now?"
"Yes."
"Then please proceed to Exit 22. A limo driver will be waiting for you with a sign bearing your name."

William thanked her and hung up. He also thanked Francisco with a two-pound tip before heading toward Exit 22.

Outside, he spotted a uniformed driver holding a sign with his name.

"Hello, are you here to take me to the hotel?" William asked.

"Yes, sir," the driver replied, opening the limo door and loading his luggage into the trunk.

"How far is the hotel?" William asked as they drove away.

"With traffic, about twenty minutes," the driver said.

"What's your name?"

"Nicholas, sir. I work with the hotel whenever they need me. For you, the limo will be available as long as you stay. That's part of the contract."

"Thank you, Nicholas," William said.

When they arrived, Nicholas added, "This is one of the best hotels in Barcelona."

Inside, the receptionist greeted him.

"Welcome, sir, may I help you?"

"Yes, my name is Dr. William Roberts. I have a reservation."

"Yes, sir. Please check this card and sign it."

William confirmed the details and signed. "Your room is number 23. If you need anything, please call the front desk. Oh, and you have some messages waiting for you."

He thanked her, then followed the bellboy with his luggage to his room.

The next morning, after breakfast, William received a message that the Director of Barcelona Hospital, Dr. Michael Rosson, would be meeting him at the hotel around ten o'clock.

At the lobby, William saw a tall man waiting.
"Hello, I'm Dr. Rosson. We spoke in France about your visit."
"Yes, I remember," William said, shaking his hand. "It's a pleasure to meet you."
"I know you've handled difficult heart cases. In fact, Spanish newspapers have already written about your operations in France. Reporters even spotted you at the German airport a few days ago."
William smiled modestly. "I just try to do my best as a doctor."

"Would you like to visit the hospital now?" Rosson asked.
"Yes, just give me five minutes to get my briefcase."

Soon, they were on their way. At the hospital, they went directly to see a heart patient, Mrs. Ana Russel. Dr. Rosson translated as William examined her. Using a special stethoscope from the Galaxies, equipped with a tiny camera, he detected two blocked veins. He prescribed medication and then asked to meet with her family.

The next day, her family met William at the hotel's meeting room. "I believe she will be fine after surgery," William explained, "though there are always risks."
Her husband asked, "How much will it cost?"
Dr. Rosson explained, "The hospital charges $10,000. The doctor's fee is $2,000."
William added gently, "Pay what you can. My priority is to help your wife."

The family was grateful and invited William to their farm after the surgery. He agreed to visit once his patient was safe.

The operation was scheduled for the next morning at 10 o'clock. William simply said, "Make all necessary arrangements. I'll be there."

 That night, William called his mother. She answered the phone, "Hello?"

"Hi, Mom!" William said.

"Hi, son, what a surprise!" she replied warmly.

"Mom, how are you, Dad, and Nolan?"

"Everybody is fine, my son. How is everything on your vacation? And how is your Aunt Rossi?"

"She's fine. Her husband and kids are very nice."

"I'm glad you had a good time," his mother said with relief. Then she added, "William, the decoration company working on your apartment is one of the best in the business. But when we called them to place the order, they said someone had already started the work. Carlos asked me, 'Who paid for it?' I thought maybe it was the distributor of office supplies for the colleges. It's a big company. I don't know who did it, but never mind, son."

William replied, "Forget about it, Mom."

His mother continued, "Also, Carlos got a call from the Hospital of Medical Supply Equipment. He told them he would be there next Monday to set up everything in the medical office. Thank you for all you've done."

"Thank you, Mom."

She added, "Nolan just got back from college. He passed his exam and will be starting again on February 6. Do you want to talk to him?"

"Yes, please."

She called Nolan and said, "Guess who's on the phone?"

"My brother William?" Nolan replied.

"Yes." She handed him the phone.

"Hi, William!" Nolan said.

"Hi, Nolan, how are you, my brother?"

"I'm fine. I passed the test and I'm in college."

"That's good. I'm so happy. I'll see you next week. Okay, bye."

When their mother got back on the phone, William said, "Mom, tomorrow I have an operation on a heart patient."

"Be careful, son. You're in a different country and they have their own laws."

"It's okay, Mom. Everybody here has been very kind."

"Well then, go eat your dinner. I'll see you soon. Bye, son."

"Bye, Mom."

The next day, two local newspaper reporters arrived at the hotel to interview William about the surgery he would be performing. The patient, Mrs. Ana Russel, was the wife of

a millionaire in Barcelona, and the media already knew
William had performed groundbreaking surgeries in
France.

Juan, a reporter from *Catalunya Barcelona Newspapers*,
spoke English and asked, "Doctor William, we've seen the
news about your major heart surgery in France. Do you
think today's operation will be successful?"

William replied calmly, "Nobody can predict the outcome
before a surgery. But I'm sure this operation is necessary to
save Mrs. Ana Russel's life. I will do my best
professionally. That's all I can say."

With that, he excused himself and left for the hospital. His
new driver introduced himself: "My name is Luis Serrano.
I'll be your driver for now. The hospital is about fifteen
minutes away."

When they arrived, reporters were already waiting outside
the hospital, taking pictures of William as he walked in.
This was to be the first heart surgery at Sant Pau Hospital
in the town of Gruinard, Barcelona.

Inside, William went to Mrs. Russel's room, where her
husband, two daughters, and the interpreter waited.

"Good morning," he said. "Mrs. Russel, are you ready?"

"Yes, Doctor," she replied.

William then prepared in the surgical room, scrubbed in,
and began the operation. It lasted five hours. Finally, the
patient was taken to recovery, and William went to the
waiting room to speak with her family.

"Everything went well," he assured them. "Tonight, she will rest. By tomorrow morning, she should be able to talk."

Her husband thanked him deeply, and both daughters hugged him. Through the interpreter, William added, "I'll return tomorrow around eight or nine in the morning."

After leaving the hospital, he returned to the hotel.

Waiting in his room was his nurse from the Galaxies, Tatty. She reminded him, "You know what to do tonight—the intervention medicine. It will help her heal quickly."

She looked nervous as she recalled how the objects in the hospital room seemed to shift when William moved his hand—something unseen by others. William reassured her and instructed her to meet him in the dining room.

Later, she arrived, a tall, beautiful blonde, drawing glances as she walked through the lobby. William greeted her, invited her to sit, and asked, "Did you bring the medicine?"

"Yes," she replied. "I have it."

"Good," he said. "Tonight, we'll apply it to her right arm. That will speed her recovery."

The next morning, William woke early, exercised in the hotel gym, and then met Tatty again. She reported, "Mrs. Russel had some pain during the night. Before she pressed the call button, I gave her pain medicine along with the intervention treatment. She opened her eyes, saw me, and then slept peacefully."

William nodded. "Good work. Let's have breakfast."

In the dining room, many guests were present, and some women glanced at William, admiring his tall, strong build, green eyes, and sharp appearance. After breakfast, he headed to the hospital with Luis.

On the way, Luis confided, "Doctor, I have two boys. One of them has asthma, and the medicine doesn't seem to work. We live just ten minutes from here."

William placed a reassuring hand on his shoulder. "When we return, take me to your house. I want to see your son."

Luis's eyes filled with gratitude. "Oh, Doctor, I've prayed so long for help. Thank you!"

When they arrived at the hospital, reporters once again surrounded the entrance, taking pictures.

Inside, William visited Mrs. Russel's room. She was sitting up, talking with her family. "How are you feeling today?" he asked.

"Thank you, Doctor," she said through the interpreter. "I feel much better. I was even able to sit up."

William checked her condition and discreetly switched the IV monitor with the advanced one from the Galaxies. He then rebandaged her chest and said, "Tomorrow you may go home, but please rest for at least three weeks. Your heart is stable now."

Her husband clasped his hands. "Doctor William, thank you for saving my wife. No one else here would have attempted this surgery. We had been preparing visas to travel to the U.S. to seek treatment. Now, thanks to you, my wife is healed."

Moved by gratitude, he added, "Doctor, when we take my wife home tomorrow, I want you to begin your vacation at one of my farms. We will take care of everything. And if you ever wish to open a clinic here, I will build it for you—I own a construction company."

"Thank you," William replied humbly.

Mr. Russel then invited him to lunch at his home. William agreed, but explained he had another patient to see first.

As he left the hospital, he told Luis, "Let's stop at the Russel farm later."

"Yes, Doctor," Luis said, smiling. "I know the way."

The limo took off from the hospital.

"Well, Louis, let's go see your boy," said Dr. William.

"Thank you, Doctor William. We need to head west for about ten minutes."

"How long has your boy been sick?" William asked.

"Well, the doctor told me a year ago that the problem was with his respiratory system. They gave him a pump that he uses every day, but I don't see any improvement. He still coughs sometimes and gets short of breath."

Ten minutes later, Louis said, "We're here. This is my home, Doctor William." He drove the limo into the driveway.

William got out as Louis knocked on the front door. His wife opened it, and Louis introduced them: "Juana, this is

Doctor William." He translated her words into English: "She says, please come in."

"Thank you, Mrs. Juana," said William.

Inside the house, George came into the living room.

"Hi, Dad."

"My boy, this is Doctor William. He's here to check on you," Louis said.

William smiled. "How old are you?"

"I am ten years old," George replied in Spanish, which his father translated into English.

"Okay, sit here on this chair," William instructed. George obeyed. "Now I want you to breathe hard for me."

William examined him while his nurse—though unseen—was also present. Louis went back to the limo and brought in the doctor's medical case. The nurse prepared some medication, gave the boy an injection, and another pill. Louis returned with more supplies, and William administered medicine for his throat.

"He'll be sleeping for about two or three hours," William said.

Juana came in from the kitchen. "Doctor William, the coffee is ready. Do you want sugar and cream?"

"Yes, please," he replied, sitting in the dining room with his cup.

Afterward, William told Louis, "It's time to get to Mr. Russell's place."

"How much do we owe you, Doctor William?" Juana asked.

"Nothing," he replied.

"Thank you, Doctor William. I will pray to my God to bless you," she said.

They left, and after almost an hour's drive, Louis said, "This is Santa Rosa Farm." They stopped at the gate where a security guard asked in Spanish who they wanted to see.

"Doctor William wants to see Mr. Russell," Louis replied.

The guard made a phone call, then returned: "Go straight to the end. That's Mr. Russell's mansion."

They arrived minutes later. Mr. Russell welcomed them at the door while his wife waited inside.

"Doctor William," Mrs. Russell said warmly, "I feel normal now. You are my angel, sent by God."

"No, no—I'm just a doctor, that's all," William said humbly.

Inside, many of the Russells' friends and even two newspaper reporters were present.

"Mr. Russell," William said, "my nurse will be here soon, if that's alright."

"No problem at all," Mr. Russell answered.

They all sat for dinner. Mr. Russell told the interpreter to offer William some wine. "This is Sangria. Would you like to taste it?"

William tried it. "Hmm, this is good."

He also tasted the food. "The meat is delicious."

During dinner, Mrs. Russell spoke through the interpreter: "Doctor William, my husband and I have been discussing an idea. If you'd like, we can help build a clinic in Barcelona. You won't need to pay anything now. Once it's ready, you can open an account and pay monthly. We want you to help many people here, as you helped me."

"Thank you," William replied. "But right now, I must open my office in my own country first. Still, I'll be in touch if I decide to open a clinic here."

Just then, the gate security called to announce another visitor. "An American lady is here asking for Doctor William," the guard reported.

"Let her in," Mr. Russell said.

Ten minutes later, a taxi arrived. Out stepped William's nurse, a beautiful blonde woman, tall and graceful. Everyone's eyes followed her as she entered the dining room.

"Good evening," she greeted, and everyone stood to reply.

Mr. and Mrs. Russell welcomed her warmly. William gestured, "Come sit here and try the food. It's very good."

She did, and soon the chef brought options for her to choose from.

After dinner, William instructed, "Nurse, please take Mrs. Ana Russell upstairs and check her operation." The two women went to the second floor.

Meanwhile, William and the other guests moved outside to the patio, where musicians played Spanish music. Tables and chairs were set, and everyone relaxed. William took two cups of wine, though his nurse barely touched hers.

The newspapermen approached. "Doctor William, how did you perform such an operation? It's the first of its kind in our country. Even in yours, it's considered extraordinary."

Another reporter added, "Are you truly from this planet? To us, you seem like a genius. That's why they call you 'the College Gene.' You're already a millionaire in your country, aren't you?"

William shook his head. "No, I'm just a doctor, and my mission is to save lives."

Later, as he prepared to leave, Mr. Russell handed him a check. "Doctor William, here is ten thousand. My wife and I will never forget you. You gave her life back."

"Thank you," William said sincerely.

The nurse, after finishing her check-up, also thanked them for the dinner. The Russells walked with William and his nurse to the limo.

"We'll see you at your office during our vacation," Mrs. Russell promised.

The limo drove off. Ten minutes later, William received a phone call.

"Hello, this is the Dean of St. George University Medical School. My name is Jeremiah Houston. Could I meet you tomorrow at your hotel?"

"Of course," William replied.

The next day, Dean Houston arrived. "Doctor William, the newspapers are full of your story. Our students would love to meet you and ask about your groundbreaking surgery. Would you visit our medical school? We'll cover your time."

William answered, "My mission on this planet is to be a doctor and save lives. I understand your intention—you want your students to reach higher goals in their careers, correct?"

"Yes, exactly," said Houston.

"Then I'll gladly visit your university. I have time tomorrow afternoon."

"Thank you very much, Doctor William. We'll see you tomorrow."

That same night, William had visitors from outer space, including his clone. They told him he needed to return to the Galaxies for two days—his biological mother was very sick.

The next day, William woke up, went down to the dining room, and had breakfast. His nurse joined him, and they chatted for a while. Later, he entered Jim's room and spent an hour there. The nurse, who had been out the previous night checking on Mrs. Rosell, told William that Mrs. Rosell was recovering quickly.

Back in his hotel room, William began preparing his speech for the St. George Medical School meeting. When he stepped out of the hotel, a man at the door asked what he needed. William replied that he was waiting for his limo driver. Within minutes, the driver arrived and parked at the entrance.

"Louis, today I need to go to St. George University," William said.
"Yes, sir. It will take about twenty-five to thirty minutes. It's on the other side of the city," Louis replied.

As they drove, Louis told William, "My son is doing so well now—he even plays in the school soccer games. My wife says you are an angel sent by God."
William smiled. "I'm not an angel. Tell your wife she did the prayers, and that is what helped. I only prescribed the medicine. By the way, I'll be leaving next Saturday for my country."
"Thank you, Doctor William," Louis said. Soon after, they arrived at the University.

At the main office, William introduced himself to the receptionist. "Good afternoon. I'm Doctor William. I have an appointment with Doctor Huston."
"Yes, sir. Please wait a moment," she replied, making a quick phone call before escorting him to the Dean's office.

"Hello, Doctor Huston," William said warmly.
"Welcome, Doctor William. Let me show you around," the Dean replied. They took a golf cart and toured the medical pavilion. Professor Elias, one of the faculty, greeted

William, saying, "It's a pleasure to meet you in person. We've read so much about you in the newspapers."

Later, William joined the staff for lunch in the dining hall, where he was introduced to everyone. They applauded his arrival. William addressed them with a short speech about legacy, compassion, and communication, encouraging the young doctors to listen, serve with love, and leave behind meaningful contributions. His words were met with another round of applause.

After lunch, William walked to Spectrum Hall with the Dean. Inside, nearly a hundred students were waiting. Dean Huston introduced him as "one of the best surgeons in France," and invited him to speak.

Taking the microphone, William shared his journey. He explained that success in medicine was not about being a "genius" but about dedication, sacrifice, and a true passion for saving lives. He told the students how he had lost his girlfriend because of the sacrifices required by his career and reminded them that becoming a doctor should never be about money or family pressure—it must come from the heart. His honesty and humility earned him a standing ovation.

Before leaving, Dean Huston handed William an envelope as a token of thanks. Back at the hotel, William packed his things and prepared for his secret journey to the Galaxies.

That night, he traveled across space and arrived at the Galaxy hospital, where his biological mother, Lest, was waiting. His clone stayed behind at the hotel, enjoying the vacation in Barcelona and attending public events to maintain William's cover.

In the Galaxies, William entered the intensive care room.
His mother was overjoyed to see him.
"Do you know the truth now?" she asked.
"Yes," he replied. "I am the Galaxy Governor's son."
She explained that his biological father had died in the war,
and that William also had a sister who served as a military
pilot. She revealed how William's embryo had been
preserved and later implanted on Earth.

William examined her heart and realized her condition was
critical. "If I operate quickly, you have a 20% chance of
survival. It's risky, but it's your best hope." His mother
agreed, placing her life in his hands. After the surgery, she
stabilized.

Meanwhile, William's clone continued sightseeing in
Barcelona, even taking a cruise, as newspapers followed his
activities.

Once William's mother was recovering, he visited a
subterranean city with his sister and friends. They toured a
frozen lake with hot springs, traveled in futuristic boats and
submarines, and dined at an automated restaurant. But
William soon returned to the hospital to check on his
mother, who handed him an envelope regarding his late
father's automobile company. William declined to manage
it, instead passing it to his sister, since he planned to remain
on Earth.

Because of the Galaxy's atmosphere, William knew he
could not live there permanently—his Earth-born lungs
were too sensitive. After giving final instructions to the
nurses, he returned to Earth, landing in Barcelona.

At his hotel, the manager gave him a global gift card from
the Rosell family as a gesture of gratitude. Soon after, the

limo took him to El Prat Airport. Along the way, Louis grew emotional, thanking William once again for saving his son. William assured him he was just a doctor doing his duty, but Louis insisted he was their angel.

At the airport gate, reporters and the Rosell family surprised him with a farewell gift and photographs. William promised that perhaps one day he would return to Barcelona. Then, boarding his Air France flight, he quietly reflected on all that had happened—on Earth and beyond.

Finally, the airline began calling passengers, section by section, to board the plane. William held a first-class ticket. He said, "Well, it's time to board the airplane," and bid farewell. The Rosell family felt saddened to see him go. William joined the passenger line, boarded the plane, and checked his seat number.

After sitting down, one of the flight attendants approached him and said, "Doctor William, I recognize you."

William replied, "Why do you say that?"

She smiled. "I've seen your pictures in the newspapers almost every day. You're very famous in this country. Even television channels talk about you. One of your patients was on TV the day she left the hospital. She told reporters that she owed her life to Dr. William Roberts. The doctors at the hospital didn't want to operate because her heart was so weak, but you injected her with special medication and operated the very next day. She said if you hadn't been there, she would have died. She called you one of God's angels sent to Earth to help the world—or at least a man with the Lord by his side.

"It doesn't matter what anyone outside the hospital says, but in my opinion, you're extraordinary. Reporters say the same—that every patient you touch seems to be cured. Honestly, it reminds me of Christ when he walked this world."

William's airplane finally landed in Paris at Charles de Gaulle Airport. After clearing immigration, he collected his suitcase at baggage claim, where many other passengers also waited. Exiting the airport gate, he was greeted warmly by his family.

"Welcome home, son," his father said. They walked together to the parking lot, got into the car, and drove home.

On the way, his stepfather remarked, "You're more famous than any movie star."

William smiled. "Why do you say that?"

His stepfather explained, "All the newspapers and television channels in Barcelona talked about you every day. Reporters even came to the house asking when you would return. Your mother and I finished preparing your office. Your grandmother redecorated your apartment, and the building now carries the sign: *Doctor William's Medical Center.* Reporters even interviewed your mother about you."

He added, "Mr. Carlos II came by yesterday asking if you had returned since you hadn't called him. I told him you'd be here today."

William replied, "I was so busy, I didn't have time to call."

His stepfather nodded. "That's fine. What matters is that you're back. Mr. Carlos II also said he's proud of you. He believes you're very intelligent, and his wife loves you like her own grandson."

"Where's Nolan?" William asked.

He went to watch a basketball tournament at his college. He'll be starting there in January," his stepfather explained.

When they arrived home, they saw reporters gathered outside. William got out of the car and said, "I'll answer your questions inside. I'm tired from the trip."

Inside the house, a reporter asked, "Doctor William, your patients say you're an angel. What do you think of that?"

"I'm not an angel," William replied. "I'm a doctor. But I do ask God to guide me in my work. To me, the human body is a temple, a vessel for the soul. My duty is to preserve life. When the body reaches its final moment, it doesn't matter if I'm the best doctor or an ordinary one—it's in God's hands. Some doctors avoid risky surgeries, but I choose to take those risks when I feel I can help. It's not because I'm an angel, but because I trust God to guide me."

The reporter nodded. "That makes you the best doctor in your patients' eyes. How many doctors will work with you in your new office?"

William replied, "I can't answer that now—maybe later. For now, I need some rest. Thank you, everyone."

After the reporters left, neighbors also returned to their homes. His mother reminded him that it was dinner time. William went upstairs, found several letters on his desk, and after reading a few, decided to take a shower. Later, he phoned Mr. Carlos II.

"Hello, William, how are you, son?"

"I'm fine, Grandpa. How about you and Grandma Virginia?"

"We're well. We need to see you as soon as possible."

"I can visit at six this evening," William replied.

Later at dinner, his stepfather mentioned, "Tomorrow, two doctors will visit. They'd like to rent offices in your building. One is a pulmonary specialist, the other is in neurology. Mr. Carlos II knows them. You can discuss it with him tonight."

After dinner, Nolan returned home. Seeing William, he rushed over. "Brother, I missed you so much!" They embraced warmly.

"How are you, Nolan?" William asked.

"I'm fine. We won today and advanced to the championship tournament."

"That's wonderful," William said.

The phone rang. William picked up. "Hello?"

"Hi, this is Grandma," Virginia said.

"Hello, Grandma. I'll be there tonight."

After saying goodbye to his family, William took his coat and drove to his adoptive grandparents' house. The maid opened the door and called out, "Mr. William is here!"

Inside, the family had prepared a surprise party for him in the patio. With decorations, music, and warm embraces, they welcomed him back. Jack hugged him with tears in his eyes. "We've all missed you, even the limo drivers ask about you. You're the number one doctor in the news!"

William examined his grandmother, who had been coughing, and prescribed medication after requesting tests. He also checked his grandfather, who joked, "Well, I feel fine, but since you're here, doctor, I'll let you examine me too." Everyone laughed, then toasted William's return.

Jack added, "Tomorrow we'll meet downtown at the new offices with the accountant and lawyer to sign papers. The building is ready with equipment, phones, and a secretary. You already have twenty patients waiting. Also, two doctors want to rent offices, and a pharmacy chain wants the corner space. It's a great start."

Grandpa Carlos reassured him, "Don't worry, son, we'll guide you. You're smart, and in two years the building will pay for itself."

Later, Mrs. Virginia's brother, Jorge, a retired judge, arrived and greeted William warmly. By eleven, William excused himself. "Tomorrow will be a busy day. Good night, everyone." He hugged his grandparents and left for home.

Chapter 15: The Inauguration

The next day, William got up early, ready to head downtown. His mother was already on her way to work at the hospital, and Nolan was returning to college for his pre-college classes. Dr. Carlos, who oversaw the hospital doctors as a coordinator, left around nine o'clock. That morning, William and his stepfather sat together at the table for breakfast.

"Good morning, Dad."
"Good morning, son."

"Dad, I was thinking… maybe you should work with me."

His stepfather raised an eyebrow. "Why do you say that?"

"Because in the office, I already have a list of nearly sixty patients."

"But son, those people want to see you."

"Yes," William replied, "but you are a general doctor. You could still help."

"Son, we'll see after the inauguration of the medical building. Be prepared—there will be a lot of people. Don't forget, even the governor will be there, along with the Catholic authorities. I read in the newspapers yesterday that this new medical building is a major development for downtown. It's the number one new medical office, and because of the location, I know the building will be fully paid off in about two years. Doctors pay high rents, and everyone prefers offices in the downtown area where they can also shop. A college friend of mine has an office just three blocks away, and he makes good money. At a meeting downtown last week, he even mentioned that if he could get a space in this new building, he would move immediately. Son, you've entered the main business district, and I believe your building will pay for itself within three years."

William nodded. "Dad, I have to do what's best for my own life. Today will be very busy with lawyers, checking everything, and signing a lot of papers. I'll see you later. Bye, Dad."
"Bye, son."

Later that morning, William arrived early at the plaza of the new building. It was the first time he had visited the site. After parking in the lot, he got out of his car and headed toward the entrance. To his surprise, a security officer immediately opened the door for him.

"Good morning, Doctor William."
"Good morning," William replied.

"My name is Robert. I'm the supervisor and in charge of all the businesses in this company. Doctor, your office is down the small hall to your right."
"Thank you."

William walked into his new office. It was spacious, with a large waiting room and all brand-new medical equipment. As he was looking around, Jack walked in.

"Hi, William."
"Hi, Jack."

Jack said, "We have to go to my father's office, the one ten Street north."

"How much time do we have?"
"Fifteen minutes."
"Let's go."

"We'll take my pickup truck," Jack added as they both walked out to the back parking lot.
"Why are we going this way?" William asked.
"Because I park in the staff lot. Where did you park?"
"In the front."
"No, doctors park on the left side of the building. When we come back, I'll show you."

They left the lot and drove north. Ten minutes later, they arrived at Mr. Carlos II's office, where a meeting was already in session.

As William and Jack entered, they greeted everyone:
"Good morning."
Mr. Carlos II stood up. "Everyone, this is my grandson, Doctor William Roberts."

He continued, "William, these two are our lawyers. They'll explain everything you need to sign regarding the building. Also, here are Doctor Angel Colton and Doctor Parker Roman. They are interested in renting offices, but since you are the owner, it's your decision."

William smiled. "Welcome, Doctors, to our medical building offices."
"Thank you, Doctor William," they replied.

William added, "Jack is currently in charge of the arrangements, so please coordinate with him regarding contracts."
Jack said, "Tomorrow we'll meet at the club with our lawyers, and you'll be ready to move."

The doctors thanked them and left. The lawyers then brought out the documents, and William began signing them. When it was finished, Mr. Carlos II handed him the final papers.

"My grandson, I promised you your own doctor's office. Here are the documents. The building is now officially yours. Jack will help guide you until you get used to running your business. I know you are very intelligent, and soon you'll have your own team working with you."

William placed the papers in his briefcase. He paused, then said, "Grandpa, thank you. You know I love you and Grandma as if you were my own blood."

Mr. Carlos II embraced him. "Jack, you are his brother, too." All three hugged, tears filling their eyes.

The lawyers excused themselves, saying, "We'll see you at lunch to finalize the tax documents."

A little later, Grandma Virginia entered the meeting room. "William, do you like your office?"
"Granny, I love it. Have you seen the apartment?"
"Not yet, but your mother told me it's beautiful."
"Yes," she said, "I was the one who directed the decorators, and all the family helped with the building. They brought in custom designs, and it turned out lovely."
"Thank you, Granny. I love you so much." He gave her a big hug.

Virginia smiled. "Carlos, I'm hungry."
"Then why don't you go with William to his apartment first? Afterward, we'll all meet at the Members Club."
"Perfect," she agreed.

William and his grandmother drove in her Mercedes. Ten minutes later, they parked in the private lot behind the building. William pointed to the gate. "Grandma, this should open automatically with a motor. I'll talk to the engineer to install one."
"Yes, have him call me," she agreed.

They took the elevator to the second floor, where William unlocked his apartment for the first time. He stepped inside, eyes wide.
"Wow… this is like a dream. It's beautiful."

"All the furniture came from my factory," Virginia explained proudly. "We make custom pieces for wealthy families and medical offices. It's one of the biggest furniture factories in the country, passed down from my father. Before I married your grandpa, my family already owned several businesses."

William looked around in awe. "Granny, this is incredible. Once I start at the medical office, I'll move in here. It will save me from traveling forty minutes every day. I especially love the desk—it's perfect for running a business."

Virginia smiled. "When I was young, I ran one of our offices. Jack will teach you how to handle the business side—he loves you like a brother."

"Thank you, Granny. I love everyone, too. By the way, did you take the medication I ordered for you?"
"They didn't have it yesterday, but they called and left a message. They said it should arrive today."
"I'll make sure Jack checks on it. You must take it as soon as it arrives—it's very important."
"Of course, son. Now let's go to the club. I'm hungry."

William drove them to the Members Club, only five minutes away. At the entrance, they handed their car to the valet and went inside. Everyone was waiting, including the local newspaper reporters.

Among the guests was Mr. Carlos II's brother, Santiago, who owned a major business in the U.K. and was very wealthy. As soon as he saw Virginia, he stood up and embraced her.
"Virginia! You look exactly as you did years ago."
She smiled warmly. "How are Rosena and your two sons? Are they here?"
"No," Santiago replied. "My older son, Sawyer, took over the airline business. He's very smart. I also have two grandsons. And now, your grandson William is making a name for himself around the world in medicine."

"In fact," he continued, "I have a major client in the U.K. who owns a laboratory. He told me he wants to contact William. Here's his business card—please give it to him."
"Of course," Virginia replied.

Turning to William, Santiago said, "Doctor William, if you connect with this man, it could be a very big business opportunity. You're young now, but by the time you reach my age, you could be a millionaire."

William smiled. "I'm ready for it."

Jack said, "Please, attention everybody. I'd like to inform you all that the Inauguration Ceremony and blessing of the building will begin tomorrow at ten o'clock in the morning. The Monsignor of St. Michael Church will be present. We will also have breakfast at eight o'clock here in this club. The Governor and the Secretary of State will be attending as well.

Tonight, the people in charge of the event will arrange seating at the back of the parking lot of the building, while we will park in the front. Mr. Soyer, the Governor, will also be there, and the front chairs will be occupied by Catholic authorities, the Governor, and his commissioners.

Kleber Square Plaza is right in the center of Downtown, surrounded by all the stores, and it usually gets very crowded during the morning hours. The Chief of Police will also be there with a group of officers to control the traffic. That is all for today, thank you."

Everybody applauded. Mr. Carlos II, who had agreed to this project with his son, said, "This is a good job." Around twelve-thirty, everyone went back home.

Doctor William spoke with Jack outside in the parking lot, near his car, about the new doctors who were interested in renting medical offices in the building. Jack replied, "Yes, they've already taken two corner offices. That means we'll have rent coming in—two thousand pounds a month. A pharmacy will also be opening on the first floor, operated by one of the Boston companies. They'll be paying four thousand pounds monthly. With this rent, you'll be able to cover taxes and some of the building's expenses. Of course, there will be management costs as well, but we only need to pay our share of the time they work in the building."

Jack continued, "We also have the third floor, which has four large offices. A petroleum company called yesterday; they want to take all of them. They're ready to sign a five-year contract at four thousand eight hundred pounds per month. That money can go straight into your reserve account at the bank. I'm sure you saw the bank papers in the folders?"

William nodded. "Yes, I'll bring the accounts from the company next week, along with the accountants who oversee all of my business. It will probably take me a couple of months to learn everything. At first, it seems overwhelming, but I'm sure I'll be able to manage it."

Jack smiled. "Exactly. Once you learn, you'll be running the business without problems. Be here early tomorrow. You and I have to take care of some things in the building before people start coming in. It's wise to be prepared for any small incidents."

"You're right, Jack," William replied. "I hadn't thought of that. See you tomorrow."

William returned to his new apartment. He organized his office desk, cleaned up a little, and made notes about what he still needed for the office. He also prepared a second room as his sacred space—a place where he could feel close to God, try out new ideas, meditate, relax, and communicate with angels.

He checked if the phone was working, but found it wasn't connected yet. He reminded himself to call the telephone company. Then, he drove to his parents' house. About half an hour later, he arrived.

"Hi, Mom!" he said warmly, hugging her. "I love you."

His mother, Lorena, became emotional. "I love you too, son."

She handed him a slip of paper. "A person called you three times yesterday. Here's the phone number."

"Thanks, Mom. I'll call later. And thank you and Dad for helping me set up the apartment."

Lorena smiled. "Mrs. Virginia loves you so much. She called me yesterday and said she'll be here this afternoon. She and I are going to Le Bon Marché to buy you blankets and curtains."

"She doesn't need to do that, Mom. They've already given me so much."

"Son," she replied, "you already have a building downtown. You have five years to pay off the remodeling, thirty thousand pounds. With the rent, the building will be paid off in just one year. At only twenty-three years old, you're already wealthy—you have a new car, a doctor's office, and soon you'll have a million-pound building paid off. God bless you."

"Mom," William said, "I saw a new development just five minutes from Strasbourg. I want to buy you and Dad a new home there."

"You don't need to, son," Lorena answered softly. "This home is good enough."

Still, William smiled. "It'll be better to be closer to me and my apartment."

Lorena then added, "Your grandmother Evelyn isn't feeling well. She asked to see you this morning."

"I'll visit her after I make a few phone calls," William said.

Later, a maid came into William's office. "Mr. William, would you like something to eat or drink?"

"Just some orange juice, thank you."

Two hours later, William told his mother, "Call Grandma and tell her I'm on my way." He kissed her goodbye and left.

On his way, he received a call from his grandfather, Mr. Carlos II. "William, we still have papers to sign. I'll keep them with me until tomorrow. And your grandmother loved the flowers you sent her. She says Thank you."

"Please tell her I love her very much," William replied.

William then drove to Mrs. Emma Louisa's house. He parked, knocked on the door, and was greeted by the maid, Martha.

"Good evening, Mr. William," she said.

"Good evening. How are you, Martha?"

"Fine, thank you. Come in. Your grandmother is outside."

When Grandma Evelyn saw him, she smiled weakly. "Now I feel better because you're here."

"What's wrong, Grandma?" William asked gently.

"I've had a headache, and my sugar is high—two hundred fifty."

William checked her heart and lungs. "You need to manage your diet better, Grandma. I'll have you admitted to the hospital for a full check-up tomorrow."

Just then, Mrs. Emma returned with her driver, Nova. She hugged William. "My son, have you grown taller, or am I shrinking?"

He laughed. "You're the same, Aunt Emma."

She smiled warmly. "You know, William, I always knew you'd become a doctor. Do you realize the entire country knows about you now? Every newspaper and television station is talking about the miracle surgery you performed in Barcelona. That woman calls you her Angel."

William looked humbled.

Aunt Emma continued, "Tomorrow, all the TV channels will be covering the inauguration. I'm so proud of you. Now, come have dinner with us."

"I've missed your meals, Aunt Emma," William admitted with a smile.

After dinner, the phone rang. It was Lorena asking him to call Jack immediately. Aunt Emma handed him the phone.

"Jack," William said, "it's me."

"William," Jack replied, "I need you at the building at seven in the morning. The inspector requires the occupancy papers before approving tomorrow's opening. Don't worry—we'll sort it out in time."

"I'll be there," William assured him.

After dinner, William stood up from the table just as Nova returned with the medicine and handed it to Mrs. Evelyn.

"Granny, you need to take two pills every day," William reminded her. She immediately took two.

Then William turned to Aunt Emma. "Let's check you now."

"I take daily pills for my heart," she said.

William examined her and noticed some swelling around her heart. After completing the check, he said, "You might feel a small pinch or a little pain." He then gave her an injection in the chest.

Afterward, he said, "You don't need the pills anymore. You'll be fine for now."

She looked at him and said softly, "Don't wonder why people call you an angel. It isn't only because you are a doctor—it's because God placed you in this world. If I could, I would join forces with the angels to save human life on this Earth alongside you."

"Well, I must go," William said.

"I'll take my sister to the hospital tomorrow morning," Aunt Emma assured him.

"Perfect," William replied. "Tell my father, and he can handle things at the hospital when she's admitted."

They all walked him to the car. William said goodbye, got inside, and drove off.

That night in his room, William received a visit from Galaxie, his nurse, and Tatty. She told him there was a major problem—some meteorites had struck part of a large city. William thought about it and told his clone that he would communicate with him the next day, and every night for the next four days, until he returned from the Galaxies.

Tatty, the nurse, brought many medications from the Galaxy's laboratory. These would be formulated and reproduced here on Earth. She would be working alongside William for a few days, though she would remain invisible. She planned to be present in the operating room whenever William needed to perform surgery—just as she did in the Galaxies.

The next morning, William woke early, went downstairs to the kitchen, and brewed some coffee. The service girl wasn't home, so he sat at the table with his cup. His mother soon joined him.

"Good morning, son," she said. "This is a big day for you."

"Yes, Mom," William replied. "Lots of people will be there, starting at ten."

Just then, his father, Doctor Carlos, walked in. "Good morning, son. Jack called me yesterday at the hospital. He asked if I would be at the inauguration. I told him I'd come around eleven, after finishing at the hospital. I'll spend the rest of the day there. And by the way, we have a big surprise for you."

"Great," William smiled. "When you arrive, just look for me on the main road in front of the ceremony."

"No problem," Doctor Carlos replied. "Your mother and I will be there. The limo will pick us up at seven-thirty."

"Okay, see you later, Dad."

William arrived at the building by seven-thirty. Jack was waiting for him with two other men. Jack opened his briefcase, spread papers across the hood of a car, and William signed them. When they were done, the papers were given to John Carlos, the building's maintenance manager. Workers had been busy all night preparing for the ceremony.

Jack then took William to the club, where guests would gather before the event in front of the building.

Soon after, William's mother and his stepbrother Nolan arrived in a limo. At the same time, three more limos pulled into the lot. Mrs. Lorena, as always, wore a warm smile.

At ten o'clock sharp, the seats in front of the new medical building were full. Reporters from various TV and radio stations were ready to cover the event.

The ceremony began with Jack Anderson, President of the Anderson Company.

"Ladies and gentlemen, distinguished governors, authorities, and honored guests," he began. "It is a privilege to stand here today at the inauguration of this new medical building. Our vision was to take a great step forward for the community by advancing medicine with a team of talented young doctors.

This building represents the highest level of modern construction technology. We only kept part of the old frame. For example, the elevator is the most advanced available on the market, the heating and air system is state-of-the-art, and security is top-notch. My father and I have built other buildings, but this is by far the most modern.

Of course, in business, there will always be competitors. Some opinions about this building have been kind, while others—let's just say—less agreeable. But opinions are like bad air: the best thing to do is open the windows and let them out for fresh air and new insight."

The crowd laughed and applauded.

"Now, I present to you Monsignor Benjie of St. Michael's Cathedral."

The Monsignor stepped up to the microphone. "In the name of the Father, Son, and Holy Spirit, amen. Ladies and gentlemen, today is a special day—the blessing of this new medical building. It is not every day that such a facility opens, one that will benefit not only our town but many beyond it.

I also know a remarkable young man who once sat in our classrooms—a brilliant student. Today, he is among the doctors leading this facility. Many of you already know him from the news. Please welcome Doctor William Roberts."

The audience rose in applause as William stood to acknowledge them.

The Monsignor continued, "Alongside him are other outstanding doctors. Together, they will make this medical center one of the best in the entire region."

He then gave the microphone to the Governor, Mr. Chase Sawyers.

"Thank you, Monsignor Benjie," the Governor began. "Ladies and gentlemen, it is a great honor to be here today. This event marks progress and history for our country. This facility will be the finest medical center, equipped with the latest technology and specialists.

I can give you a personal example: my mother-in-law suffers from heart problems, and my brother-in-law had to take her all the way to London because we lacked specialists here. This new center will change that.

I also bring good news: as Governor of Strasbourg, along with the Senate, we have agreed to grant a tax exemption of four thousand pounds per year for the next five years. This will allow more resources to improve this facility even further. Congratulations to the owners and everyone who made this possible."

The audience applauded warmly.

Next, Mr. Carlos II stepped forward. Everyone rose to their feet in applause.

"Ladies and gentlemen," he began, "I'm not much for speeches. Usually, someone else does that for me because I'm a businessman. But today I must say a few words.

One of the greatest blessings in our family has been my grandson, Doctor William Roberts. He gave me the idea for this center when he was still in medical school. Let me tell you how it began.

Years ago, I collapsed at a train station. I don't remember much, but this young man saved my life. Within minutes, I was breathing again. He insisted I take medicine, even though I told him I felt fine. That night, I invited him to my home, and from then on, he became part of our family.

Since then, William has cared for all of us. My wife struggled to walk for years until William treated her. Today, she is well. My brother, who smoked heavily and had a chronic cough, was also healed after William treated him. He is here today to personally thank him."

The crowd clapped.

Mr. Carlos continued, "William never cared about money—only about helping people. That's his true quality. In fact, we already have a list of sixty patients waiting for him, plus many others for the specialists joining this facility.

This medical center will be one of the busiest in the region, led by three remarkable doctors: Doctor Joshua Loan, Doctor Cristian Long, and the brightest of them all—Doctor William Roberts."

He paused, smiling proudly. "Now, I think I've spoken long enough. Let us hear from my grandson, Doctor William."

William's Speech and the Opening of the Medical Building

"Thank you, Grandpa, and thank you, ladies and gentlemen. It is an honor to stand here in front of all of you. I also give thanks to God in Heaven for making me the person I am today. Many things happen in our lives—sometimes you sit alone and realize that you are ready to face the next day. Time is often short, and we don't always stop to think about the good we did the day before.

Some of you may have heard the word 'angel.' People sometimes call doctors angels. But really, I only do what must be done, and that happens in everyone's life. I once read in a newspaper in Barcelona, Spain, about a French doctor who performed heart surgery. The patient called him an angel because, at that moment, they believed God's angels worked through him.

It is like climbing a mountain—sometimes the climb is too steep, and the burden feels too heavy. But faith, and the help of God's angels, can lighten that load. The higher you climb, the easier it becomes, and when you reach the top, the air is clear and fresh.

That is how I see my work. I believe in God, and my patients often have great faith too. Together, that makes healing possible. From tomorrow onward, I will dedicate myself to serving everyone who comes to these medical facilities. Thank you very much."

The audience rose and applauded. Soon after, the Governor, Mr. Chase Sayers, along with Monsignor Father Benjie, arrived at the front entrance. Together, they cut a large ribbon, officially opening the Medical Building. Reporters and guests cheered as the doors opened.

Afterward, William, Jack, and Mr. Carlos II met with William's parents. "Mom, Dad, I'm starving," William laughed, and Jack agreed. They all walked to the limo, and the driver took them to *Jack's Dinner Place*, a restaurant inside the club parking lot.

Seated at the table, they enjoyed a long-awaited meal. William looked at his grandparents, tears in his eyes. "Grandpa, Grandma Virginia, I don't have words to thank you for opening the path to my future. Because of you, I stand here today." He embraced them, and everyone at the table grew emotional. William's mother also hugged them and added, "I thank God for giving you both long life to see William's progress. I know it has always been your dream, just as it was mine when he was younger."

Later, William told his parents, "I need to head back to my new apartment and make sure the cleaning staff did their job. Tomorrow, I'll move in my belongings." His mother felt a little sad, but William comforted her. "Don't worry, Mom. I'll probably see you every day at the hospital." She nodded, smiling through the emotion. "I know, son. I won't hold you back. Every mother feels this way when her child's wings are ready to fly, but I'm so happy to see you independent."

When William arrived at his building, movers were unloading medical equipment for the new doctors. He inspected his apartment when his phone rang—it was Jack.

"Hello, William. I forgot to mention—tomorrow my wife will be your first patient. She hasn't been feeling well."

"What does she have?" William asked.

"Just a cold, I think."

"Jack, I'll come over tonight to check on her."

"But William, you must be exhausted from today."

"Jack, you're my family. Don't you know that?"

"Fine," Jack replied warmly. "I'll see you soon."

Half an hour later, William arrived at Jack's house. The service girl opened the door and led him to the living room. Soon, Lilian, Jack's wife, came down the stairs, smiling.

"Hello, William. How are you?"

"I'm fine. How about you?"

"My body aches, and I have a headache."

William examined her carefully. "I can hear some issues in your lungs. Are you having trouble breathing?"

"Yes, this morning I felt a heavy weight on my chest."

"Then I'll check your heart too. You'll need a prescription. Take this medicine and these pills, and I'll check you again tomorrow."

Just then, Rossi, the service girl, came in with coffee. "Doctor William, I know how you like it."

"Thank you, Rossi," he said with a smile.

As he reached for the cup, Jack entered, kissed his wife, and said, "See, Lilian? That's my brother William." Everyone laughed.

"William, don't go back to your place tonight," Jack insisted. "Stay here. We have a guest room. Tomorrow is your first day at the office. Consider this your home, too."

That evening, after dinner, Jack's daughters came home, kissed their parents, and greeted William warmly. They spoke about their day playing tennis, and William encouraged them: "That's great. Sports keep you healthy and strong. Remember, everyone has an angel guiding them—you just need to listen closely."

Later, Rossi brought the evening medicine for Lilian, who took it gratefully. William reassured her: "This will help you sleep." Soon after, everyone went to bed.

The next morning, William woke early, showered, and went down for coffee. Rossi greeted him kindly before he left for his apartment and the medical building. At nine, he began his first official day at his new office. Patients filled the waiting room, and with Nurse Tatty's help, William treated them tirelessly until midday.

After work, exhausted, he visited his parents' home for dinner. "Dad, I need help," William admitted.

Doctor Carlos smiled. "I'll take a week off to help you, son. And I know a young doctor at the hospital who can assist you long term. He'll be a great addition."

That evening, Dr. Carlos called the young physician, Dr. Jason, who agreed to meet William the next day. William felt relieved. "Now I can focus on my sickest patients first. Thank you, Dad."

Back at his apartment, William completed patient files and organized them for his new nurse. Just as he tried to rest, his Galaxie mother appeared. She handed him a massive laboratory book and spoke of diamonds she once owned on Earth, tied to her past.

"Son," she said, "life here is short compared to ours in the Galaxies. Once you marry here, you will lose the secret to travel between worlds. Only if you marry a Galaxie girl can you live with us—but even then, only for a short time."

William listened quietly. She promised to return soon with legal certificates to secure the diamonds in his name.

"Thank you, Mother," William replied softly.

Then she vanished, leaving him with the heavy knowledge of his two lives—one on Earth, the other tied to the Galaxies.

Chapter 16: The Heart of a Healer

The next day, Dr. William woke up and began preparing for the new workday at his office. Just as he was getting ready, his phone rang.

"Hello!" he answered.

"This is your grandpa."

"Hi, Grandpa, how are you?" William replied.

"I'm fine. I'm arranging for a doctor's helper. Not yet, but your father will be working with us for a week. Also, a young doctor has shown interest in this job."

"Do you need me, Grandpa?" William asked.

"Well, my brother is in Paris in the hospital. If you can, please go and see him—he has heart problems. Jack is on the way to your office."

"Okay, Grandpa. My father will be there around ten-thirty. Tell Jack to meet me in my office, and then I'll go to the hospital to see your brother. I'll see you later. Goodbye, Grandpa."

"Bye, son, and thank you."

After the call, William continued getting ready and left his apartment. He had about an hour before starting work, so he drove to a nearby restaurant for breakfast. As he parked, he noticed Jack arriving at the same time and parking in the space next to his car.

Inside, William was already seated at a table when Jack walked over.

"Hi, William."

"Hi, Jack. Did my father call you?"

"Yes, it's about my uncle Santiago. I think he had a heart attack."

"Well," William said, "my father will be in my office at about ten-thirty. I'll wait for you there, and then we'll go to the hospital."

"Alright," Jack nodded, "I also need to send some deposit money to the bank. I'll see you later. Bye."

After finishing his breakfast, William paid the waiter, left the restaurant, and drove back to the building.

By the time his father arrived at the office, the waiting room was already full of patients.

"Son, there are so many patients here," Dr. Carlos said.

"Yes, Dad," William replied. "We only take about twenty a day, but today is an exception. Still, I have to leave for an emergency—Jack's uncle, Mr. Santiago, is in a Paris hospital. You'll need to handle today's patients."

They both walked into the waiting room, where William addressed the patients.

"Ladies and gentlemen, I have an emergency to attend to. This is my father, Dr. Carlos. He will see everyone today, and afterward, you will follow up with me. Thank you."

Jack arrived, and soon he and William left for the hospital.

They reached the Pitié-Salpêtrière Hospital and went to the second floor. At the front desk, they asked for Mr. Santiago Alberton and were directed to Room 24.

Inside, they found him sleeping. Jack gently called, "Uncle Santiago."

He opened his eyes and smiled faintly. "Now all will be well. Here is Dr. William."

"Why do you say that?" William asked.

"I know you are a good doctor. But I ask you—do you have your sacred room ready at home, a place where you can pray to God in peace? That room is where you must always open your soul, seek healing, and ask for divine inspiration."

"I always pray to God before working with any patient," William reassured him. "Now let me examine you."

After checking him, William said, "You need surgery for your heart veins. Two of them are blocked. But I recommend a hospital transfer to the Centre Hospitalier Universitaire of Limoges. I'll prepare the paperwork and give it to them."

Jack agreed, and the two said their goodbyes to Santiago before returning to William's office.

Later that evening, William's father went with him to his apartment, which was large and spacious—almost like a house. Just then, the phone rang.

"Hello," William answered.

"This is Mom."

"Hi, Mom, where are you?"

"I'm in the parking lot. Is the office closed?"

"Yes, we closed at six. You said you have two nurses with you?"

"Yes. Their names are Leah Eaton and Lucy Ezekiel."

"Alright, park inside. Turn at the corner street and enter through the gate in the middle. I'll meet you there."

William went down to meet his mother and the two nurses.

"Son," Mrs. Lorena said, "this is Leah and this is Lucy."

"Pleased to meet you both," William said warmly. "Let's go up to my apartment."

They all took the elevator to the second floor, and within twenty feet, they reached his apartment. Once inside the living room, the nurses greeted Dr. Carlos.

"Hello, Dr. Carlos," they said, recognizing him from their hospital days.

"Hello, girls," he replied. "Are you ready to work for my son?"

"Yes," they answered together.

"My father will brief you tomorrow," William said. "He'll explain the daily duties."

Meanwhile, Mrs. Lorena busied herself in the kitchen, making coffee for everyone. Soon, they were all seated in the living room, drinking and talking about the new building.

"This apartment is very modern," Lucy observed. "And the furniture—it looks so expensive. Everything here is new."

After the coffee, Mrs. Lorena said, "Come with me, nurses. I'll show you the office where you'll be working. I know it well—Dr. Carlos and I designed it."

"Thank you, Mom," William said.

While his mother toured the nurses around, William discussed plans with his father. Just then, the phone rang again.

"Hello, this is Dr. William."

"Doctor, this is the Centre Hospitalier Universitaire. The patient, Mr. Santiago Alberton, has been transferred here. He is in Room 19."

"Thank you. I'll be there in one hour," William replied.

Later, his mother returned from the office. "I've explained the nurses' duties. If you want to make any changes, they are ready."

"That's fine, Mom," William said.

"Well then, I must leave. Nolan will be home tonight from college, and there's no one at the house right now," she said, leaving with the two nurses.

"Good night, Mom. I'll call you later," William promised.

Dr. Carlos also stood. "Son, it's time for me to go home as well. I'll see you tomorrow at nine o'clock. The accountant will be here to prepare payroll papers for the new employees. Make sure you tell him the nurses' salaries and hours. And remember—you'll be earning just like any other doctor here. You'll also be training the nurses."

"Alright, Dad," William agreed.

As his father left, William reminded him, "Tell Mom I'll be at the hospital tonight. I also need to talk to Grandma."

An hour later, Dr. William Robert arrived at the hospital. He went to see Mr. Santiago and his wife, explaining the procedure for the operation and how it would be done. He reassured them, saying, "There may be some risks, but don't be nervous. I am optimistic that everything will go well. I'm focusing on the bright side, not on the negatives. What's most important now is gratitude, expectation, and trust."

He then began his examination. Having Santiago lie on his back, William used his special stethoscope, which he reserved only for cases requiring surgery. "You'll feel a small pinch in your chest," he said as he injected medication. He also instructed the nurse to connect an IV line to Santiago's arm. "The night nurse from Galaxies will also monitor you."

Mr. Santiago nodded. "I'm fine, Doctor. Do whatever has to be done."

William finished and said, "I'll let you know later what time I will operate on you tomorrow. The nurse will check on you tonight."

Leaving the room, he went to the hospital doctor's office to make the necessary orders for the operation. He wrote a note for the nurse on duty to ensure Santiago would be monitored throughout the night. After completing the paperwork, William returned to Santiago's room with documents for approval.

"You'll be in the operating room at 8:15 in the morning," William explained. "Is that alright with you?"

"Yes, Doctor," replied Mrs. Santiago.

Their son, Greason, stood up, hugged William, and said, "Yesterday, my Uncle Carlos II told me, 'My grandson William is the best doctor in all of France.'"

William smiled. "Not the best in France, but I do care for my patients as if they are my own family."

He wished them goodnight and left the hospital. At the entrance, he was unexpectedly approached by a reporter from *Le Populaire* newspaper of Limoges.

"Dr. William, are you performing surgery on Mr. Santiago Alberton?"

"Yes," William replied. "But I'm sorry, I need to get home now. I'll speak to you tomorrow after the operation. Thank you."

That evening, Mrs. Lorena had just arrived home. The two nurses parked their cars in her driveway, said goodnight, and left. Inside, Nolan was already home.

"Mom, I love you," Nolan said, hugging her.

"I love you, too, son. I've missed you."

"I've missed you as well. How's William doing?"

"He's fine. Why don't you visit him tomorrow? He'll be glad to see you and show you his apartment. But call him first."

"Okay, I'll do that. I've got all my dirty laundry ready, too. Tomorrow, the cleaning man will bring the clean clothes and pick up the rest. Just put your laundry in the box in the garage, mark it with your name, and place your smaller clothes in the hamper. The service girl will handle it—she does laundry every Tuesday."

"Alright, Mom, I'll take care of it."

Soon after, Dr. Carlos came home. Nolan greeted him with a hug. "Dad, I love you."

"I love you, too, son. How's college?"

"Great. I made the Dean's List, and my science professor praised my work."

"Congratulations," Dr. Carlos said proudly.

In the kitchen, Mary, the service girl, asked Mrs. Lorena, "Shall I serve dinner?"

"Yes," Lorena replied, then went to the living room where her husband was resting.

"I'm tired, Lorena," Dr. Carlos admitted.

"It must have been a long day. Lots of patients?"

"Yes, but more than that, I did a lot of driving. William really needs a doctor to help him—twenty patients a day is too much."

"You're right. And with so many people on the waiting list, it will take two months before things settle down."

Mary then announced dinner was ready. After washing up, the family gathered at the table. Nolan said the prayer, and they ate together.

Later that night, William returned home. In the kitchen, he found his mother talking to Mary.

"I'm home," he said. "I've missed your cooking."

Mary smiled and quickly prepared his dinner. Ten minutes later, she placed it on the table. "Your dinner is ready, Dr. William."

"Thank you, Mary."

After eating, William joined his family in the living room. Nolan came down the stairs and embraced him. "My brother!"

"My younger brother," William said warmly. "How's college?"

"Very good."

"I'm glad to hear that. I need to make a phone call."

He went upstairs to Nolan's room and used the phone to call his grandmother and Aunt Emma Louisa.

"I saw the newspaper today," Aunt Emma said. "You'll be operating on Mr. Santiago Alberton—the millionaire from the UK. I knew back when you were in high school that you'd become a great doctor."

"Thank you, Aunt Emma. How are you feeling?"

"I had my heart checked because of high blood pressure. It was too high."

"Tell Nova to bring you here tonight. Stay at Mom's house. I want to see you."

"Alright, I'll be there around 10 p.m."

"Good. I look forward to it."

Just then, the phone rang again. Jack was calling. Mrs. Lorena answered, then handed the phone to William.

"William," Jack said, "the Health Department will inspect the medical offices tomorrow. They'll issue the certificate for display, but there are also some documents you need to sign. John Carlos, who oversees the building, told me you must be there."

"Jack, I can't make it. I'll be in surgery with your uncle at eight in the morning. Can we do it the next day?"

"As long as a doctor signs, it's fine."

"My father will be there at 9 a.m. He can sign the papers."

"That works. Thank you, William. Goodnight."

Afterward, William made two more calls, then gave instructions to Nurse Tatty to prepare Santiago at the hospital.

Later, Mary brought coffee for everyone. Nolan told William, "I'll visit your office tomorrow."

"Yes, I'd like that," William said.

Mrs. Lorena added, "It would be better after 5 p.m., when the office closes."

"That's fine, Mom," William said. "He can come anytime. I'll give him the apartment keys, and he can wait there until I'm finished."

The doorbell rang. Nolan opened it to find Mrs. Emma Louisa and Mrs. Evelyn, their grandmother.

"Come in, please," Nolan said.

"Hi, Mom. Hi, Aunt Emma," Lorena greeted them warmly, hugging both.

William embraced his grandmother. "I love you, Grandmom."

Everyone gathered in the living room, then William took Aunt Emma upstairs to Nolan's room to check her health.

He measured her blood pressure and listened to her heart with his special stethoscope.

"Your heart is fine, but your cholesterol may be high. I'll inject some medication to lower your blood pressure. Let me know tomorrow, and I'll prepare a prescription. Nova can pick it up at the office."

"Don't worry," Aunt Emma said. "Tomorrow, I must go to the hospital to renew a contract for medical supplies. I'll also stop by your office."

"Thank you, Aunt," William replied, as they returned downstairs.

"I must head home now. I have to leave early tomorrow," she said, hugging everyone goodbye.

Grandmother Evelyn stayed for the weekend.

Meanwhile, at the hospital, Nurse Tatty checked in at the front desk on the second floor. After signing in, she went to Mr. Santiago's room.

"Are you Dr. William's nurse?" Santiago asked.

"Yes," Tatty replied. "I'll be preparing you for tomorrow's surgery."

She injected IV medication designed to open his veins in advance. This was the same advanced treatment used in Galaxias, a medicine not yet available on Earth. Dr. William and his legal team were in the process of securing the patent. Once approved, the drug would be produced in UK laboratories and sold to hospitals. Mr. Carlos II, William's adoptive grandfather, already had the paperwork ready for production. No one yet knew how successful it would be, but it was expected to become a breakthrough in medicine, though very costly and limited to hospitals.

The next day, Doctor William arrived at the hospital. In the parking lot, several reporters from the U.K. and Limoges newspapers were waiting near his car. One of them asked, "Doctor William, how does Mr. Santiago feel about this operation?"

"He's doing very well," William replied.

"How long will the surgery take?" another asked.

"It's hard to say exactly—probably around three hours. It depends on what happens once we're in the operating room. Well, fellows, I must go now. I have a patient to operate on. Thank you."

Inside, William went to Mr. Santiago's room. "Good morning, Mr. Santiago. Good morning, Mrs. Santiago," he greeted them. "How is everyone today?"

"We're fine," they replied.

"Are you ready, Mr. Santiago?"

"Yes, Doctor, I am okay," Santiago answered.

"Then I'll see you in the operating room," William said.

Nurse Tatty was already there, assisting. The surgery took four hours, but there were no complications. William managed the blood flow to the heart with great skill. Still, he knew the hospital's equipment was far behind what he had used in the Galaxies. There, advanced machines made such procedures easier and safer, while here they relied on a limited bypass system that lacked certification and speed. William had performed the same operation in the Galaxies with far more control.

He had been working with medical engineers from the Galaxies, and if he could bring their technology to Earth, it would revolutionize surgery. But the cost would be enormous. He was waiting for the financial means to make such instruments available on this planet.

After the procedure, William left Mr. Santiago in the recovery room and went to the cafeteria with Nurse Tatty. As they ate, she told him about the train accident she had once experienced while traveling to her work in the Galaxies. Two older doctors soon approached William's table.

"How can someone as young as you perform such an operation without the proper equipment?" they asked.

At the next table, Doctor Rolon overheard and spoke up. "It's in his genes. Haven't you read the newspapers?"

William smiled modestly. "Any doctor can do it, provided they have the Lord on their side and know how to control blood flow. That's something I first learned in medical school."

The doctors listened but remained skeptical. "It's easy to say that," one remarked before returning to his work.

William and Tatty went back to the recovery room. Mr. Santiago, half-asleep, asked the nurse for a cup of water. She checked with William first.

"Yes, give him some water," William said before leaving. The nurse remained in the room to care for him. In the Galaxies, she herself was a doctor, but here she served as his nurse.

"I'll see you later," William told her.

"I will too. Goodbye," she replied.

William hurried out of the hospital to return to the office, where his father was attending patients. But reporters were waiting outside once more.

"How is Mr. Santiago doing after the operation?" they asked.

"He's fine, resting in recovery," William answered quickly. "Now I need to get back to my office. Thank you."

At the office, William relieved his father. "Okay, Dad, take a break," he said.

The nurse brought in the next patient—a seventy-five-year-old woman with respiratory problems. William placed an oxygen mask on her and examined her lungs. Finding an issue in the right lung, he told her daughter, "I need to inject some medication. It will sting a little, but she'll feel better by tomorrow."

The daughter agreed, and soon after the injection, the woman was breathing easier. Ten minutes later, she went home.

Meanwhile, William's picture appeared in every major newspaper in France and the U.K. One headline even called him *"The God of Doctors in France."*

William's half-brother Nolan was studying at the Czech Technical University. William was very proud of him; in three more years, Nolan would graduate as an engineer. He had even helped Nolan with college tuition.

By this time, William had completed two years of office practice. Now he mostly worked in the operating room, as his other business responsibilities left him little time for general practice. His father, now retired from the hospital, served as head doctor in the office, while Mrs. Lorena also worked there, leaving her hospital position for this new role.

Whenever possible, William still traveled to the Galaxies to help in their hospitals. He was considered one of the top doctors there as well, specializing in heart surgery. After his first year in private practice, William had trained two assistant doctors who now supported him, allowing him to focus mainly on surgeries. He also owned a medical laboratory in the United Kingdom—GlaxoSmithKline Laboratories—where his medicines were manufactured.

Eventually, William succeeded in bringing Galaxy medical engineers to Earth. Under assumed identities, they worked as international students, but in reality, they were designing instruments never before seen on Earth. Two of these advanced devices were already built and in high demand by hospitals, though extremely expensive. A waiting list had formed for those eager to acquire them.

By now, Doctor William was already a millionaire and the most famous doctor in France. Sadly, his grandmother, Isabella Roberts, in the U.K., passed away in her sleep from a heart attack. William traveled to her funeral. His biological mother from the Galaxies had left him a large inheritance, including diamonds worth one million pounds.

After a trip to Africa to transfer the assets, he deposited them in France and used part of the money to pay off the medical building account—just as his mother had wanted.

Around this same time, King George VI of the U.K. died, and Queen Elizabeth ascended the throne at a young age. Reading the newspapers one day, she saw an article about William. Curious, she told one of her attendants that she wished to meet the famous French doctor.

Thus, William received an official invitation to Buckingham Palace following his grandmother's funeral. The Queen welcomed him with a reception and spent two days hosting him at the palace. One of the princesses, whose name was withheld to avoid publicity, was especially drawn to William. Handsome and renowned, his visit was widely reported in U.K. newspapers, with pictures of him alongside the Queen.

Back in France, William's medical business flourished. He partnered with pharmaceutical laboratories, releasing several prescription-only medications. His adoptive grandfather, Mr. Carlos II, retired and set off on world travels with his wife. His son, Jack Alberton, now ran the laboratory business, maintaining William's partnerships and growing the operation into a multimillion-pound enterprise.

Meanwhile, in southern France, William invested in the Haute Bourgeoisie, planning two luxury homes in one of the richest towns. His sister from the Galaxies, Miatrt—a high-ranking commander in their air forces—gifted him a special spacecraft disguised as a helicopter. It could land on his medical building's roof, but for safety, he planned to store it on a mountain farm. Outwardly, it appeared to be a normal helicopter, complete with Earth registration papers, but once beyond the atmosphere, it transformed into a spaceship equipped with advanced defenses, invisibility, and unmatched speed.

William also entrusted his sister with managing factories in the Galaxies that had belonged to their biological father. Though they loved him dearly, he could never stay in the Galaxies for more than a year, or he would rapidly age, appearing as if over a hundred years old. To survive there, he required protective clothing. His nurse, Tatty, also his girlfriend, faced her own challenges—she could not live permanently on either planet. Every six weeks on Earth, she needed to leave the atmosphere to recharge her energies. Despite this, they cherished each day together.

Two months after Mr. Santiago's surgery, William attended Jack Alberton's birthday party. To his surprise, Mr. Santiago and his family were also there. Rising from his seat, Santiago hugged William and said, "Thank you—you saved my life. Here is a check for £10,000 for your charity hospital. I learned how it helps those who cannot pay their medical bills, even the homeless. Son, you're not only a great doctor—you also have a great heart."

Carlos II added, "I told you, Santiago—William is a humble man. He never tells us about these things."

Jack smiled. "I knew, Dad. The accountant told me about the charity."

Mrs. Virginia, William's grandmother, said, "My grandson, I knew long ago the kind of person you are. When you were in college, I saw a newspaper picture of you saving a young boy run over by a car. You performed a tracheotomy on the street, and the ambulance arrived minutes later. The doctors at the hospital said whoever had done it had saved the boy's life. Reporters searched for the student responsible, but no one came forward. William, I knew it was you."

"I was just in the right place at the right time," William replied. "It's my duty to save a life if it's in my hands."

At the party, many wealthy young women admired William, drawn to his reputation and good looks.

Later, William purchased a farm outside the Vosges. There, he built a high-roofed garage to house the special helicopter. He completed the necessary paperwork to register it in France, though it contained Galaxy serial numbers. Since the law required official registration, he complied. Having taken flying lessons and earned a pilot's license, William could fly it safely, though the spacecraft itself was far beyond Earth's technology.

Over three years of practice, William's business grew steadily. He paid off his medical building and acquired two large homes—one for himself and one for his mother, Lorena. He still used his apartment during the week, keeping an office there as well. His pharmacy line expanded across France, connected with his laboratories. His father, now fifty-five, trained another doctor to take over office duties, while a CEO managed William's broader enterprises. Jack often advised him in business matters.

One day, William was surprised when his grandparents visited his office as patients. "Why didn't you call me?" he asked. "I would have come to your home."

"We wanted to feel what it was like to come to your office as patients," they replied.

William smiled and treated them, giving his grandmother medication. His grandfather told him, "I knew from the first day you were destined for this. You are already a famous doctor and millionaire. Thank you for honoring your grandfather's guidance."

They reminded him of their upcoming fiftieth anniversary and invited him to the celebration.

Meanwhile, Mrs. Lorena continued to manage the office, a role she enjoyed. William's downtown office became one of the most modern in the country. Using Galaxy's knowledge, he developed advanced medical instruments, some with electronic functions, making him not only a famous doctor but also a recognized genius in the medical field.

Despite his success, William remained humble. Alone, he often spent time in meditation, receiving mental images and insights. He believed imagination and thought shaped human experience, and through quiet reflection, insights grew like seeds into understanding.

Though wealthy, William's heart never changed. He invited Aunt Emma Louisa to Saint Michael's Church in his old hometown. After the service, they had breakfast together.

"I remember working for you in the old warehouse," William said. "It needs repairs now."

"I might have to close it," she admitted. "The roof is failing. I found another warehouse downtown, but I'm waiting to hear from the owner."

"Aunt Emma, that warehouse is yours, isn't it? I want to help you. You treated me like a mother when I needed it most."

Tears filled her eyes. "I did it because I believed in you. Even in high school, I knew you were different—too smart to waste your gifts."

Moved, William hugged her. "I will never forget you."

He revealed that he had already arranged for a construction company to build her a new warehouse. In the meantime, she could use a rental one. "Here is the contract," he said. "The company will call you tomorrow."

Overwhelmed, Aunt Emma thanked him. Mrs. Lorena added, "He will never forget what you did for him."

Emma replied, "Your real father would be so proud of you."

Later, Emma recalled seeing a woman on television who had been helped by William's charity insurance after surgery. Without it, she would not have been able to pay her hospital bills. "Your mission on Earth is clear, William," Emma said.

William nodded. "My mission on this planet is to save lives—whenever God gives me the opportunity."

Chapter 17: Full Circle

One month later, Doctor Carlos Phillis, who had officially retired, came downtown for his farewell party. The celebration was hosted by Grandpa and Grandmom Virginia at the Downtown Club. All the doctors from the hospital where he had worked attended.

At the party, Doctor William addressed the crowd. He spoke with deep gratitude about the man who had played such an important role in his life:

"When I was fourteen years old, he married my wonderful mother. I believe it was God who put him in my path. We adjusted to our new life easily, and with my half-brother Nolan, we became one big family. Since that day, we have always been happy. As a college student and later as a doctor, he stood by me as a father. To me, he *is* my real father and always will be. He was there when I needed a father, a friend, and a guide through medical school. Today, I am proud to honor him with this award—as a father and a college partner—and present him with a retirement bonus of £20,000. Come down, Dad."

Doctor Carlos Phillis took the microphone with tears in his eyes. "I am the luckiest man on this planet," he said. "I began a new family with my son, and I have never been happier. My wife, Lorena, worked so hard to raise her son without a father. And I, in turn, gained a son when he had no mother. Thank you, my son, and thank you to everyone here tonight. This beautiful party will remain an unforgettable memory in my life."

Doctor William and his girlfriend were also preparing for their wedding. The celebration was set to take place at his farm, with Mrs. Emma Louis overseeing the arrangements and Mrs. Lorena handling the details. This event was reserved only for family and close friends. Tatty, his bride-to-be, would have to present herself like a normal Earth woman.

Two weeks later, they married. Their honeymoon was in Spain, a gift package from the Alberton family grandparents. Among the guests were William's biological mother, sister, and a few close friends from the Galaxies. Everyone admired the breathtakingly beautiful bride. The next day, the couple left for the Canary Islands.

During the trip, William often wore a hat to avoid being recognized by reporters. But two days before they returned, one of his former patients spotted him on a tour bus and alerted the press. Jorge, a reporter from Santa Cruz, approached him.

"Doctor William, you are so famous! Three years ago in Barcelona, you performed a heart operation for the Rossell family. They call you the 'Doctor's Angel.'"

"I am not an angel," William replied humbly. "Just a regular doctor."

The reporter turned to his wife. "And now, your beautiful wife—what is her name?"

Tatty smiled. "I am Tatty."

"Thank you," she added politely. "But we must go."

Meanwhile, Doctor Carlos Phillis enjoyed his retirement. He no longer needed to work, had a comfortable home, and looked forward to seeing his son graduate as an engineer in another year. William's medical practice was thriving. The building was now fully paid for, and due to high patient traffic and parking issues, two of his fellow doctors had relocated to another office downtown. William quickly filled the vacant space by hiring two more doctors. He also purchased two old houses near his clinic to expand parking.

Not long after, Mr. Carlos II fell very ill with heart problems and was hospitalized. He was placed on a ventilator while Jack and Grandmom Virginia stayed at his side. William treated him with IVs, medication, and injections in the lungs. Eventually, his grandfather's condition stabilized, and he was able to breathe on his own again. William firmly advised him to stop drinking wine for at least a month, and afterward, only one glass a day.

"Grandson," Carlos said, "I knew you would say that to me."

"I love you, Grandpa," William replied. "I want you to stay healthy."

Jack, meanwhile, had begun to notice Tatty. "She is so beautiful," he remarked. "And young!"

William smiled. "She's from the U.K. I met her and her family while traveling to Manchester. She lives with her uncle in Limoges and works with me in the operating room. She's practically another doctor."

Jack teased, "Sounds like you're in love with her."

Grandmom Virginia added warmly, "Go ahead, son. She *is* very beautiful."

William only smiled. "We are good friends." In truth, they had no idea she was Tatty from the Galaxies. The two planned to marry both in the Galaxies and on Earth.

During a short vacation, William visited his biological mother in the Galaxies. She lived in a mansion equipped with solar power and special generators since sunlight was scarce there. Robots assisted her at home, and she was content. William saw family photos, including his biological father—blond, with blue eyes—just as his sister had described. Now, William finally believed it.

He learned more about the three races that lived across the Galaxies—each intelligent, technologically advanced, and culturally unique. Unlike the stereotypes imagined by people on Earth, they were not "green and ugly," but humans with delicate bodies adapted to their environment. On Earth, the oxygen levels affected them differently, which was their main distinction.

Back on Earth, William was deeply in love with Tatty. Advanced medical equipment allowed her to adjust to Earth's atmosphere so she could live and work as a normal nurse, traveling home to the Galaxies only once a month.

Soon, they married in a grand celebration hosted by his biological mother, who was also expecting another child. While William was in the Galaxies, a clone filled in for him on Earth to avoid suspicion. Upon his return, he immediately resumed treating patients.

Among them was Mrs. Sabrina Aubrey, whose heart was very weak. William was prescribed medication for a month, planning to reevaluate for surgery afterward. Another patient required vein treatment before undergoing an operation, while a third, Christopher Jace—a wealthy

French businessman—needed urgent heart surgery. Initially operated on by another doctor, Jace nearly suffered a heart attack, and William had to take over. His intervention saved the man's life, though he required rest afterward.

Another patient was admitted with severe lung problems. William discovered a blockage in the left lung and urged an immediate operation to save the man's life. With the hospital's new advanced equipment, William successfully removed small tumors and restored the patient's health. His family was overjoyed.

One of the hospital doctors who observed William's performance became curious about his unusual stethoscope. Unlike a normal one, it contained an internal camera that allowed William to see inside the body during surgery. After the operation, Doctor Xavier Janson, the head of the hospital, asked to speak with him.

"I admire you, Doctor William," Janson said. "How can someone so young perform surgeries that no one else can? I went to medical school too, but you—are you even human? Some say you are a genius. Others whisper you are an alien."

William smiled calmly. "Doctor Janson, I was born here on Earth. My father was a ship mechanic, and my mother was with him when I was born in the middle of the ocean, on their way to South America. I live here in France. If you wish, I can show you how I work. Perhaps we can perform a surgery together someday."

Doctor Janson shook his head. "No, thank you. I prefer only to observe. But I still cannot believe you are from this planet."

It wasn't the first time people suspected William of being otherworldly. But Earthlings had little understanding of the Galaxies. In truth, Galaxian people were not monsters—only humans with more delicate systems and superior technology.

Despite the doubts and jealousy of others, William carried on with his mission. He saved lives, mentored young doctors like Luke Mario, and inspired patients and colleagues alike. The newspapers began calling Luke his protégé, noting that under William's guidance, he had already performed two successful surgeries. Still, whispers lingered among some jealous doctors, especially Doctor Janson, who remained convinced William was not entirely of this world.

Mrs. Lorena fell sick, and William's stepfather called him. After finishing the phone call, William got ready and went to his mother's house, which was only two blocks away. He brought her to his own home, where she was running a fever.

This was the first time she met Tatty, William's nurse. She was instantly fond of her, looked at William, and said with a smile, *"My son, she is beautiful. How long has she been working for you?"* William replied, *"Mother, she only works as a hospital nurse, mainly in the operating room. She is as skilled as a doctor and an excellent nurse."*

At that moment, his brother Nolan returned home from university and said, *"Our mother is here with me now. I know she'll get well soon, especially under your care."* He hugged William and added, *"Brother, I need to get back to university. I have my final exams this week."* William reassured him, *"Don't worry, I will take care of Mom. Just give me a call once you reach the school."*

The same day, William's stepfather had to travel to New York at noon. His mother, who was already in Manhattan, had fallen sick as well. His brother Ethan Phillis took her to stay with him for two months, but she also grew very ill and was admitted to Presbyterian Lower Manhattan Hospital.

William loved his mother deeply. He also knew that this might be the time she would come to better understand who he truly was. She trusted him but had always suspected that there was something different about her son. Since he was twelve years old, when she witnessed him heal their old neighbor, she had sensed he had a gift — something beyond a normal boy.

Now, William put her into a deep sleep to rest. At the same time, his biological mother, Saatrine, arrived to see her. She was preparing to take Lorena to the Galaxies. William and Tatty stood by her side as Saatrine piloted the spaceship to their destination. Upon arrival, William placed his mother in a hospital in the Galaxies. She had vein problems in her heart, but for William, the surgery was simple with the advanced medical equipment available there.

The next day, Lorena woke up in the recovery room. Looking around nervously, she realized she was in a place unlike any hospital she had ever seen. *"Where am I?"* she asked anxiously. William comforted her, *"You are in a hospital, Mom."* Tatty brought her a drink and said, *"Here is your juice, and this is your breakfast."* Lorena tasted it and remarked, *"This is delicious."*

William explained, *"I performed the operation here, Mom. In the Galaxies, surgeries are done differently. We use lasers to make the incision, and after the procedure, special tissue-like staples are used to close the wound. Another*

*laser is applied, which softens the skin tissue and heals it
completely within minutes. There are no scars left behind,
so no one even knows an operation was done."*

As Lorena rested, a blonde lady entered the room. William
introduced her, *"Mom, this is Mrs. Saatrine."* Saatrine
shook her hand warmly and said, *"It is a pleasure to finally
meet you."* Lorena noticed that William's features
resembled hers. Saatrine then spoke:

*"You don't know me, but I saw you twenty-three years ago
in Manchester when you had just married William's father.
You were married for two years but could not conceive
because your husband had fertility problems. My own
husband and I traveled from the Galaxies, as he was at risk
during the war. To preserve his lineage, we implanted his
embryo in you. Nine months later, you gave birth to
William. From that day, I have always returned to Earth to
check on him. You may not have known, but deep down you
must have sensed he was different."*

She continued, *"Do you remember the day your husband
lost his job after drinking too much? Your father and sister
took you to France to see Uncle Saturn, who owned a
hardware store in Limoges. And do you recall your Aunt
Emma Louise, the wealthy singer? Everything connects
back. Lorena, you are truly William's mother — you
carried him in your womb and raised him. But biologically,
he is also my son."*

Both women hugged William tightly. Lorena said, *"Yes,
this is our son."*

The next day, William and his sister — a military major —
took Lorena to Saatrine's castle. It was like a dream to her.
She had never seen such beauty: robots working in the

house, modern cities with flying vehicles, supermarkets that operated completely automatically. She was fascinated and whispered, *"I never imagined such a world could exist."*

Two days later, Lorena awoke from a dream and told William, *"I dreamed that you are from another planet and that this lady is your biological mother from the Galaxies. But to me, you will always be my son."* William laughed and replied, *"Maybe my father was from another planet, but you are the only mother I know and love."*

Soon after, William received a long-distance call. It was Doctor Carlos. *"Hello, son, how is everyone at home?"* William answered, *"We're fine, Dad. Mom was sick for three days, but she's better now."* Carlos asked to speak with her. Lorena took the phone, saying, *"Hi, sweetheart, I am feeling better now. I just need to stay in the hospital a little longer, but soon I'll be home."* They also talked about Nolan, who had just been featured in the newspapers for his remarkable engineering project.

Nolan was preparing to graduate from the Czech Technical University on May 15, 1973. His project — connecting Folkestone, England, with Coquilles, France through an advanced electric channel — had already attracted government attention. His graduation was celebrated with a party at the Downtown Club, arranged by William's grandfather, Carlos II.

Meanwhile, William completed his new garage. His sister brought him a spaceship that could transform into a regular helicopter, though it required special fuel units from the Galaxies due to Earth's temperature differences. The ship ran on solar power, which was still a futuristic concept on Earth at that time.

Emma Louise's warehouse was also completed. At the inauguration, she hugged William with tears in her eyes and said, *"This is a dream for me. Everything here is modern — even the alarm systems and forklifts. Son, this must have cost you a fortune."* William replied, *"Aunt Emma, for you, this is nothing. You are like a second mother to me."* Both were moved to tears as reporters and city officials covered the event.

Later, William's grandmother hugged him and said, *"My grandson, you are the best blessing a grandmother could have. God has surely chosen you to help others. Downtown, the homeless thank you every day. I saw one of them on TV saying that thanks to your charities, they now receive food and even medical care."*

When a reporter later asked him if he felt proud of himself, William replied humbly, *"I am not proud. I only feel grateful that I can help those who need it. That is my mission on this Earth — to serve God and anyone who needs me."*